The Two Loves of
Will Shakespeare

The Two Loves of Will Shakespeare

A NOVEL BY

LAURIE LAWLOR

Holiday House / New York

Library of Congress Cataloging-in-Publication Data

Lawlor, Laurie.
The two loves of Will Shakespeare / by Laurie Lawlor.— 1st ed.
p. cm.
Summary: After falling in love, eighteen-year-old Will Shakespeare, a bored
apprentice in his father's glove business and often in trouble for various misdeeds,
vows to live an upstanding life and pursue his passion for writing.
ISBN-13: 978-0-8234-1901-2 hardcover
ISBN-10: 0-8234-1901-0 hardcover
1. Shakespeare, William, 1564–1616—Juvenile fiction. [1. Shakespeare, William,
1564–1616—Fiction. 2. Great Britain—History—Elizabeth, 1558–1603—Fiction.]
I. Title.
PZ7.L4189Tw 2006
[Fic]—dc22
2005052537

To all lovers of Shakespeare past,

present, and future

The Two Loves of
Will Shakespeare

Chapter One

In the low, woody Midland hills, bonfires winked like baleful eyes across the valley. The sweet smell of woodsmoke and the strident sounds of singing and wild carousing filled the air. All of Warwickshire seemed awake on Midsummer Eve—the shortest night of the year.

A restless crowd had gathered beside the Avon River outside of town. Along the reedy shore young men teased and joked. Young women laughed and shrieked.

"How now, how now, mad wag!" shouted one young man. "It's almost midnight."

"Come out of the darkness. We're growing bored, Will," another warned. "How long must we wait to see your secret?"

Some of the bystanders jeered. Others whistled. A few, who had grown tired of leaping over the bonfire, sat in the grass or stared into the flames with a kind of stubborn expectation. This was the night that fairies could speak with human voices. This was the night that certain blooming flowers, when picked, promised everlasting bliss. Anything was possible.

When the high keening sound began, the crowd grew quiet. "You hear that?" someone whispered.

"Perhaps it's wind in the trees."

"Must be witches."

"Who goes there?" shouted Hal. He was a stout-bellied bald man who clutched three bottles of sack. "Nephew, is that you? Give us some sign, Will."

Suddenly the strange noise stopped. A light bobbed in the darkness of the river. The torchlike flame appeared to hover over the water. It grew closer and closer.

"Who gabbles so monstrously?" a loud, clear voice demanded. "Have you no respect for your betters? Know you not the Justice of the Queen's Peace?"

"Sir Lucy," Hal warned the others in a rough whisper. "I can scarce believe my eyes. He's walking on the water."

The crowd murmured with fear and apprehension at the sight of the powerful, puritanical squire gliding along the surface of the Avon. "God save us," they whispered. "God save us."

"To think some gentlefolk from Charlecote was just like Christ crossing the waves in the Bible."

"Keep your mouth shut, fool."

The young men doffed their caps and bowed in panic. The young women made short curtseys and scuttled into the shadows as if to hide.

"You, sir. The fat, rude one, speak up," called the floating figure in the large hat and cape. In one hand he held a long staff with a flame burning at the top. The torchlight flickered eerily and cast a great shadow, so that the man's face remained concealed beneath the hat's brim. "How is it that you doubt my presence?"

"I don't suspicion you, sir," Hal said. Awkwardly he pulled his dirty cap from his head. The bottles clanked in his trembling arms. "I see you plain as day, sir. You are a fine gentleman."

"Is it not true that three freshwater fish appear on my family's coat of arms? Three luces rising to the surface. I am simply doing the same." He made a few elegant strides.

"Don't mean any disrepair, your honor," Hal mumbled. "A luce, sir, must be terrible clever."

"Do not confuse a luce with a louse," the voice boomed.

Someone in the crowd tried to stifle a chuckle.

"Yes, sir," Hal replied. Something of his old bravado had returned. He took a few steps closer to the water's edge as if for a better look. "Will, can that be you?"

The crowd hooted with delight and relief. "Come, coz!" one of the young men shouted and clapped his cap back on his head. "You gave us a bad scare."

"Aye," said another, laughing heartily, "what a jest! How'd you do it?"

"Better not let Sir Lucy catch you!"

Will tried to keep from smiling in triumph. They had believed him so completely. For a few brief moments he had filled them with wonder and terrified them nearly witless. Recalling the sense of power made him shiver. "What disrespect, what riot do you rabble dare incite?" Grandly, he moved the burning end of the staff back and forth and tried to regain the sensation of moving, speaking, thinking like haughty, dangerous Sir Lucy. "How dare you abuse a gentleman? Even one who smells as fishy as I do. Do you know that I could have you whipped, hanged, drawn and quartered? Don't think I have not heard your insolent singing."

"What singing, your most powerful pompous honor?" Hal said and winked at the others. The young women giggled.

Will shuffled his feet, which were attached at the soles to timbrels. The small, flat drums, tied carefully under his bare feet, were becoming damp but still managed to keep him afloat as long as he maintained his balance. "You know the ballad I mean, Sir Sack-and-Sugar."

Will cleared his throat and steadied himself with the burning staff, which rested on the water on another timbrel. "The offending song goes like this," he said, and began to sing in a fine voice:

"If lousy is Lucy, as some folks miscall it,
Then Lucy is lousy whatever befalls it:
He thinks himself great,
Yet an ass in his state
We allow by his ears but with asses to mate.
If Lucy is lousy, as some folks miscall it,
Sing lousy Lucy, whatever befalls it."

The crowd clapped nervously. Even in the darkness of Midsummer Eve, when everything seemed turned upside down, someone might be listening. Someone might report them. Reckless Will grinned and bowed and bowed again, savoring the peril as if it were the finest, strongest, sweetest sack.

Later, when he returned to shore, Will pulled the

timbrels from his soggy feet and threw down the wide-brimmed hat and heavy, sodden cape. His friends thumped him heartily on the back. "Well done, Will!" Hal said. "Your jest had me baited and hooked. Just to show you I'm a forgiving fellow who don't take no officiousness, here's a bottle I owe you."

Will uncorked the sack and took a long swig. "You're a generous, honest gentleman, Uncle," he said, and grinned.

"Aren't you the Lord of Misrule!" exclaimed Mopsa, the barmaid from the Swan. She threw her arms around Will and held him in a viselike grip. "Give us a kiss."

"Marry me, Mopsa!" Will said, and gave her a loud smack on the cheek. Everyone laughed.

Mopsa blushed and let him go. "Your pranks is going to find you at the gallows one day."

"Many a good hanging prevents a bad marriage," Will replied lightheartedly. He took another long swig, grabbed Mopsa by the hand, and pulled her to a more secluded spot along the river. She giggled with delight as he coaxed her into the tall prickly grass. In the darkness of Midsummer Eve, he told himself, weren't all women beautiful?

"You love me, don't you, Will?" Mopsa said. Her

coarse hair brushed across his face, enveloping him in the smell of smoke and yeasty, stale ale.

He laughed and sat up. His shoulders slumped forward. The power he had experienced while play-acting seemed to have completely seeped away. No matter how hard he tried, he could not recall the exhilaration of walking on water. He could not recall the thrill of being a fine gentleman. He was himself again.

Sparks from the nearby bonfire rushed toward the starry sky as yet another load of wood was tossed into the flames. Will's friends cheered. His uncle howled with laughter.

"Will?" Mopsa said. She pulled him toward her. Her calloused hands moved with a kind of urgency she seemed to think might please him. "Ask me again, but say it proper this time."

He kissed her to make her quiet. Her skin tasted salty. She had a familiar, forgiving plumpness that comforted him the way he was comforted by a soft feather bed or a haunch of well-cooked venison.

He kept kissing her, going through the motions of delight, yet all the time he heard the chuckling of some demon in his ears. "*Something is wrong.*"

She pushed him away and sat up. Against the fire

he could see her lift her strong arms to replace the coif on her head and tie the laces under her chin.

"Not leaving so soon?" He reached up and playfully tugged her hair before she could tuck it back inside the cap again.

She swatted his hand away. "A rogue and a liar and a blasphemer. That's what you are."

"Not I!" he protested.

"You say you love me. You say, 'Marry me.' But you don't mean it."

"Such babble. Kiss me, Mopsa."

"No." She sighed. "If you loved me, you really would marry me. No more dodging in fields and stables and haystacks. We'd be a proper married couple."

Will rose on his elbow to better observe her amazing performance. She could not be serious. "What about the others?"

"What others?" She pulled her greasy kirtle down so that the skirt hem covered her bare thighs.

Will counted on his outstretched fingers. "Every single one of my friends. Then there's the constable, the baker, the shoemaker, the smithy's idiot son—"

"They meant nothing," she interrupted. "That was before you."

Although her flattering words amused him, he managed to bite his lip to keep from smiling.

"You think I'm gastful." She bent forward, her shoulders shook, and she made a whimpering sound.

"Don't cry," Will begged. He couldn't stand the sound of her sobbing. It made him feel guilty. "You know I can't marry. I'm apprenticed still."

She sniffled loudly, hiccuped, and wiped her face with her sleeve. "You could promise me. When you're not assigned anymore, you'll marry me."

"Nonny, nonny," he said in a soothing voice. With one swift movement he slipped his arms around Mopsa and expertly lowered her flat onto the ground again. She protested, then laughed good-naturedly as he pressed his face into the hollow of her neck and kissed her over and over again.

His drunken friends chattered and hooted around the fire. What were they laughing about? The way he'd fooled them into thinking he could walk on water? He longed to hear their praise, their distracting stories and jokes. The mournful melody of a lute floated and shimmered across the river. Now a lone tenor voice echoed with a love ballad. Wind gusted and the flames crackled and lurched higher.

"Will?" Mopsa's sudden voice clawed the air like a cat.

"Don't talk." He had to concentrate. He kissed her with exaggerated enthusiasm. Stubbornly, he fumbled and caressed, trying to ignore the heat surging from the bonfire and the shadow that sniffed around him like a lurking black dog. His thoughts strayed to all the lost, honest lovers in the woods who were embracing and oblivious to everything but each other. *And where am I? Here, haunting the outskirts of the wilderness—alone, unblessed—unable to pretend otherwise.*

With his usual quick efficiency he finished his lovemaking. It was perfunctory and uninspired. He blamed the hour. He blamed the place. He blamed wandering malevolent Midsummer spirits—even as he heard a tired sigh inside his head whisper, "*Try, try again.*"

Mopsa giggled. She stood up and shook the grass from her apron. Will paid no attention to her soft, fawning entreaties. He stared into the distance as a wheel big as a man and bound with straw was set afire and rolled down a hill. The burning circle bounced and shimmered in the darkness. Brilliant as the sun in descent, the wheel rolled faster and faster until it toppled over and the light was suddenly extinguished.

While the crowd cheered, whistled, and shouted with delight, Will felt only a growing sense of sadness. Summer had reached its peak of light and warmth and abundance. After this, the days would grow shorter and the darkness would increase. He was eighteen years old and his life—stale, unprofitable—seemed to be slipping, slipping away. No matter how many fires were lit, he had the sinking feeling that his youth, like the brightest season of the year, would soon be over.

Mopsa leaned over and whispered with fishy breath, "Farewell, my love." She tenderly kissed him on the top of his head.

"*'Tempus edax rerum,'*" he replied in a solemn voice.

She gave him a puzzled look. "What?"

"'Time, the devourer of all things.' It's from *Metamorphoses*."

"Who?"

"Nothing. Nothing."

"Oh," she said. "Tomorrow, then?"

Will nodded absentmindedly, all the while studying his friends, who cavorted and wobbled numb and pain-free in the firelight. He could have been just like them if he'd never discovered Ovid and the writing that enticed and transported him. His life would be so much easier if only he'd remained ignorant of the world inside books. "I should kill that schoolmaster," he mumbled.

"Oh, Will," Mopsa said gaily. "You already sound like a jealous married man!"

"What?" He looked up at her, annoyed. *Why doesn't she go away?*

"Behind the tavern, don't forget. I'll be waiting." Mopsa waved her hand and disappeared into the mob of dancers whirling and stamping, twirling and jumping in the light of the fire. Their mouths seemed frozen, like the grins of skulls or the tormented lips of lovers at the height of passion.

Will rubbed his eyes to shake off the vision. Then he stood, slipped his arms into his rumpled doublet, and adjusted his breeches and the hose covering his legs. He grabbed the bottle his uncle had given him and strode over to his friends. They pranced and lurched to the rhythm of the lute music. "Drink!" Will shouted in a too-loud, too-jovial voice. "Lads, let us drink!"

"Though I look old, yet I am strong and lusty!" Hal said in a slurred voice. He grabbed the bottle and took a greedy swig. "They say dragons hate the stink of burning bones, Nephew. That is why we toss branches forked like rib cages and branches thick as thighbones into the blaze. The fire and smoke's what drives away dragons that poison the wells."

Will snatched the bottle from his merry-cheeked uncle. He tipped it back and allowed the burning liquid to pour down his throat. This night Will was determined to get drunk, very drunk. If he could not chase away the dragons with fire and smoke, perhaps he could drown them with spirits.

Chapter Two

Two days later a second miracle occurred. A dwarf-sized man dressed in a fawn-colored tunic with slashed sleeves and trappings of red and green satin pranced across Clopton Bridge. On his head he wore a red wide-brimmed hat, and on his feet were long, pointed red shoes. With every dancing movement the little man set off a startling chime of music. Attached with leather fasteners around his arms and neck, wrists and elbows, knees and ankles, were hundreds of small, glimmering silver bells that shook when he moved his arms, stomped his feet, or wiggled his ankles.

The load of bells seemed too heavy for one so small, and yet he pranced effortlessly. Now his arms sang. Now his legs. In one hand he carried a long staff, nearly twice his height, decorated with bells and long, soiled green, yellow, and red ribbons. He used this jingling staff as a weapon to scare off growling dogs and bold children who tried to pelt him with pebbles.

A crowd gathered. No stranger came to town without close inspection. And this little man was certainly the most original lunatic anyone had ever seen. Fearlessly, he made his way among heavy carts, roaming pigs and cattle, and squawking chickens.

"All his body's dressed like a maypole," marveled one woman.

"Aye," said another, and winked, "or Tom O'Bedlam's cap, for he seems surely mad."

"Looks to be devil's work," replied a third, who scurried away to alert the authorities.

Curious townspeople lined Fore Bridge Street. Over their arms hung baskets heavy with cabbages, bread, or live chickens. Bundles hastily tied with old rope rode on bent shoulders. Slack-jawed, the crowd watched the strange music-maker skip and cavort around piles of dung in the muddy road. He didn't look the least bit happy. He made a scurvy face and drew his mouth awry, as if in deep concentration.

The man's child-sized body appeared to be made up of mismatched parts. His head was too big, too old and his legs were too strong, too thick for one standing no taller than a young schoolboy. In a loud, sending voice he called, "Earl of Worcester's Men a-coming!

Edward Alleyn this afternoon from London! Edward Alleyn a-coming!" With each syllable he shook a different part of his body, and a different chorus of bells sang.

News traveled quickly from shop to shop and across garden walls. The seventeen streets and lanes of town were so close-set with two hundred and seventeen houses, it wasn't necessary to lean far from an upstairs window to hear or spread the word whenever traveling mummers, minstrels, bear-baiters, jugglers, or jesters came to town from London, one hundred and twenty miles away.

"Edward Alleyn!" called the harness-maker's wife to her neighbor across the lane.

"Who?" replied the draper's maid.

"They say he speaks his part prately. A clever player he is."

"Clever enough for me if he moves his arms like windmills and struts and shouts. Them's the only ones I go to hear."

Soon the whole town rumbled with the news that the Earl of Worcester's Men would perform that very afternoon at the guildhall in a special performance before an audience of the high bailiff and all the aldermen. If the players met with the government officials' approval, they'd receive a license allowing them to perform for the general public the following day in the outdoor courtyard of the Swan, the inn on Back Bridge Street.

At the glove shop of Will's father on Henley Street, there'd been only three customers all morning. Yet Will had already heard every detail of the players' arrival. Excitedly, he decided to catch a glimpse of the famous Alleyn as he passed through town. Escaping from the shop, however, would not be easy. Although his father had gone down the street for a pint of ale at Attwood's, Will must reckon with his sister. Thirteen-year-old Joan followed his restless pacing around the dusty shop with the attentiveness of a fierce-eyed gargoyle.

Will untied his apron.

"Where do you think you are going?" Joan demanded. She looked up at him from the work-bench, where she stitched together four pieces of pale leather to make a glove. Like all glove sewers, she had purposefully grown long, strong fingernails on her first finger and thumb in order to tuck in the fourchettes, thumbs, and quirks—all parts of the glove itself. Her thick yellowish fingernails darted back and forth between glove parts like the tough beak of an angry bird.

"Don't scowl so, Beauty. What say you to this?"

Will folded his arms across his chest and began a series of complicated dance steps. He kicked and hopped until dust rose from the floor. "Badger taught me. He said in London fine gentlemen call the dance's tune, 'I Loved Thee Once, I Love No More.' Now you try."

She smiled. "Not I, you rogue. I cannot dance."

"Oh, fie. Yes, you can." Will hoisted Joan to her feet so quickly that the new glove she was working on went flying. He twirled her around and around.

"Stop! Stop, rascal!" she said, laughing.

"You see? Nothing to it. Now I must be on my way."

"Sirrah!" she said, and dizzily sat down on the bench again. She blinked as if she'd just inhaled the greeny burning-of-lye stench from the tanning pits behind the shop. "What excuse do you have this time? We'll never finish the gloves for Quiney if you're always stepping out. Don't think Father hasn't noticed."

"I'll be back before he returns."

She picked up the fallen glove. "I have heard such promises before."

Will glanced out the unglazed window that opened onto noisy Henley Street. He watched nervously for the bobbing head of their returning father. Flies buzzed above the worktable piled with pieces of tanned leather and their father's tools: long shears, round paring knife, and narrow French rule. Will ran his finger along the pattern that his father had made but not yet cut in the kidskin, which felt as soft and yielding as the nape of a woman's neck.

"I must be on my way," Will said. "Be a dear, sweet sister and make up some excuse for me. You know I'd do the same for you."

"Would you? I will hold you to your promise," she said slyly. "Before you vanish, tell me where you're going."

"To see the players arrive, what else?" Will stuffed the apron behind a half-dozen tawed, or cured, skins of sheep, goats, horses, and deer stacked on the shelf. He dashed out the shop door, glad at last to have escaped.

Will hurried past their neighbors: the tailor; the smith, who forged prisoners' chains; the miller; and the woolen draper, who kept beehives in his garden. He hurried past the crowded baker's house, with seven squalling children, and the mercer's, with eight sons and six daughters, each tougher than the next.

Safe walking through town demanded swift reflexes. Nimbly he dodged a rooting pig, two lounging beggars, a mob of scavenging dogs, and a pair of stampeding horses. With one eye skyward he remained vigilant of falling objects—the putrid contents of slop buckets, dishpans, and chamber pots dumped from upstairs windows. He breathed only through his mouth to keep from smelling the stench of dung heaps and piles of rotting garbage.

"Good-day, Will!" called the haberdasher's youngest daughter. She trudged behind her father, who led a lame horse.

"Such radiance!" Will made a low, dramatic bow, then did a few outlandish dance steps. "I loved thee once, I love no more."

The girl, barely twelve, giggled with delight. Her blush made her plain, horsey face seem almost attractive for a moment.

"Stay away from him, girl!" her father barked, and gave Will a threatening look. "He's a dawcock. You hear?"

Will had to try very hard to keep from laughing as he hurried on his way. "Dawcock. Dawcock," he repeated with satisfaction.

At the corner of Wood and High streets, Will nearly ran headlong into John Bramhall, the church warden. Fortunately, before an actual collision could occur, Will darted behind a cartload of hay. The bishop's righteous henchman was on his daily rounds of rooting out sin and terrorism against the Church of England. Busily, Bramhall peered at a newly posted sign on the wall of the tavern. "Ungodly blasphemers!"

He ripped the paper from the wall as if it were sin itself. He crushed the sign, tossed it onto a dung heap, and marched away.

Curious, Will crept closer. He picked up the torn paper and eagerly read what was left of the advertisement for the Earl of Worcester's Men:

spectacle in 9 episodes...
ship battle, dissipation of rebel...
great triumph of fighting... gentlemen at
barriers... divers souls wonderfully descrived
in their several torments...

Everything about what the theater company planned on performing sounded exactly to Will's liking: plenty of action, spectacle, and great triumph of fighting. Somewhere in the distance a crowd cheered. Will sprinted toward the sound.

Chapter Three

Will reached High Street just as the parade of actors made its way south toward the guildhall. Townsfolk shouted, "Huzzah!" and applauded with delight. Will pushed through the throng to get a good look at Edward Alleyn. Where was he? Will scanned the dozen players. They beat drums, blew horns, and waved their hats with broken, dirty feathers. "Come the morrow if that we may," they called in unison, "at six of the bell, we 'gin our play."

At the head of the parade swaggered a tall actor very different from the rest. In his black velvet jerkin, yellow doublet with ruff and wristlets, red cape, and blazing green satin hat, he hailed the crowd with the assurance of a prince. This, Will decided, must be Alleyn. Who else would own boots of such fine white leather? Who else would sport a sword with a silver hilt and a matching dagger hanging from his belt? Who else would wear costly leather gloves that reached nearly to his elbows? Each glove was embroidered at the cuff with metal threads and spangles that glinted in the sunlight.

Will studied the face of Alleyn, who appeared no older than he was. There seemed nothing remarkable about Alleyn's features. He had a high, expressive forehead, dark eyebrows and hair, and a wispy actor's beard. Will touched his own chin to check his growing whiskers. *No better than mine.*

When Alleyn passed Will, he lifted one gleaming gloved hand, smiled, and beckoned. At that moment, Will felt something akin to the prickly static of a cat's fur when petted backward. Alleyn's lightning gaze shot past Will, darted among the simple farmers, tradesmen, and yeomen, and somehow transfixed each of them with a mysterious force that would both outrage and terrify Church Warden Bramhall. Watching Alleyn work his magic made Will understand for the first time why the church feared players.

Suddenly the ox herder's brawny son shoved his way into the street and tried to snatch Alleyn's dagger. Everyone was too shocked to stop him. With surprising swiftness Alleyn kneed the startled young man in the stomach, slammed him against the wall, and held the blade to his neck.

"Do you wish to die, scum?" Alleyn boomed in a voice as potent as a summer thunderstorm.

The crowd hushed. Nothing held townsfolk interest so well as a bloody fight or a good hanging.

"Speak!" Alleyn demanded.

The young man trembled. His eyes rolled back into his head for a moment. And then, to the crowd's surprise and disappointment, Alleyn stepped away and let him go free.

"Weren't real!" the ox herder's son crowed, and rubbed his thick, dirty neck. "Weren't a real sword."

Alleyn ignored the comment. He turned and, with a flourish, began the procession again. Desperately, Will pushed and shoved his way along Chapel Street to Church Street to catch another glimpse of Alleyn. When he reached the corner of Tinker's Lane, a bottleneck of gawkers piled up in the narrow passageway. "Now what?" Will grumbled. He elbowed his way closer to the front and discovered that the little man with the bells was being held to the spot by Bramhall.

The grim-faced spy gripped the little man's staff and tried to wrest it from him. "How dare you come here looking like the devil? Begone, stranger, before the bishop sends you to prison."

The little man refused to be threatened. "Let go!" he cried. The bells shimmered and shook.

The crowd muttered sullenly. Bishop Whitgift was a feared man who'd already sent hundreds of townsfolk to the stocks or prison in the five years since he had been appointed by the Queen to preserve and protect the purity of the Church of England. Last year the fine for refusing to go to church had been raised to twenty pounds a month—a sum no one could afford.

Any individual who said or heard mass in the tradition of the Old Faith was punished with confiscation of property and livestock, and long terms in prison. Neighbors turned in neighbors, prompted by spies like Bramhall, who prowled in search of those who might dare hide Romanist priests, celebrate feast days, say rosaries, or revere other Catholic relics kept secret in their houses.

"Wanton abomination!" Bramhall shouted at the dwarf.

"Let go, I say!" the little man bellowed. He kicked the church warden hard in the shins. The bells pealed. The crowd cheered.

"He's got bottom," someone said.

"Aye, real spirit for such a wee fellow," replied another.

The little man took a swing at Bramhall and barely reached his waist. Bramhall stepped back, unhurt. The crowd tittered softly, then became silent, as if afraid someone of importance might take down their names for treason.

With a fierce, implacable look the little man glared at the church official towering over him. The unfairness of the match outraged Will. Without thinking, he stepped forward. "Let him go, sir. He's not hurting anyone."

"Who dares speak?" Bramhall demanded. With contempt he scanned the crowd.

Will nearly shrank away under the church official's wrathful stare, then he remembered Alleyn and the way he'd fearlessly held a lout by the neck with nothing more powerful than a sword made of lathe and paint. "I spoke, sir," Will said loud enough for everyone to hear.

Bramhall's eyes gleamed like a glover's shears. "What's this? The stubborn recusant's son telling *me* what to do? You and your family should have been fined and imprisoned long ago. Your father is a Catholic and a traitor. Everyone knows—"

"With all respect, sir," Will interrupted. He clenched his fists. "This player has done no one any harm."

The crowd barely breathed.

"The devil," Bramhall said in a loud, pious voice, "comes in all forms, all sizes." He paused. Just as he was about to open his mouth to continue his sermon, something hit him in the back of the head. His hat flew off. As Bramhall bent to retrieve it the little man grabbed the staff and planted a ringing thump on the back of the church warden's bare head.

"Ow!" Bramhall screamed, and staggered.

The little man turned to Will and stuffed something into the front of Will's doublet. "Keep this safe."

Will had no time to reply. Someone punched him in the neck. He turned, grabbed the nearest arm, and shoved his victim's face down into the mud. A general pushing match erupted. Fists flew.

Old Faith followers, long persecuted, joined in with vigor. They punched and throttled Protestants who had invaded their holy places, chopped the heads off statues of the blessed Virgin Mary, and stolen Saint Aelred's girdle, a precious relic said to help women through childbirth. Old Faith followers kicked neighbors who'd whitewashed paintings of miracles and pulled down their rood lofts where holy statues once stood. They pummeled Protestants who'd exiled holy water, chalice, and font, and sold the sacred vestments of the church to aldermen's wives to make carpets and bedclothes. And it wasn't long before the strict-line Protestants jumped into the fray, intent on defending themselves against the wicked Catholics and the Protestants who weren't pious enough.

Will kept swinging, not caring which religion he knocked senseless. He slugged and elbowed with great abandon. Never once did he notice the actors scurry away. They were led down an alley by the jingly little man, who wisely seemed to sense that public disturbances like this would certainly ruin their cause with the bailiff and possibly damage their few remaining intact costumes.

When the constable arrived, the fight abruptly ended. Will and a dozen other usual suspects— mostly young men his age with a taste for blood whenever the opportunity arose—were rounded up and marched to the jail on High Street. On their way they viewed the stocks for drunkards, swearers, abusive and violent persons, and other mean delinquents. They trudged past the ducking stool for fraudulent traders and scolds and the branding irons used to punish sheep stealers.

Will held his cupped hand over his bloody eye and grimaced with pain. His clothes were filthy and torn. He and the rest of the prisoners were herded into a cell, where they squatted on the hard-packed dirt floor. Will didn't bother to try to talk to any of his fellow brawlers. He sat cross-legged, deep in miserable thought. He should never have left the shop.

Fitfully, he dozed off, hunched against the damp stone wall. Suddenly he was shaken awake. He looked up and saw his father's furious red face staring down at him. "Get up, worthless drevyll," Father growled, and kicked him as if he were nothing but an imbecile kitchen servant.

Will staggered to his feet. He glanced at the other prisoners, who seemed surprised to see him dragged out of the jail cell. Will stumbled beside his father outdoors into the blinding daylight. His eye was swollen and crusty with dried blood. Even though his father was nearly a head shorter than Will, he walked fast and with determination. He was a square-built man with long arms and a shocking, pincerlike grip. Roughly he tugged Will by the ear, then cuffed him hard on the back of his head. Sharp pain spread through Will's scalp. He knew better than to cry out.

Every time they passed a neighbor or another merchant, Father gave Will another hard slap. Will tried not to look at Father or the neighbor. He kept his arms up to shield his face. He knew from past experience exactly how his father was looking at him at this very moment. He was looking at Will as if he were an inferior trank—a piece of leather absolutely good for nothing. It was this look, this glance of total disappointment and disapproval, that pained Will more than any punch, any gouge, any kick.

When they rounded High Street and headed west on Henley toward home, Father kept sharp hold of him. "Such disobedience!" he complained loudly when they passed Mistress Hornsby. "Impudent ungratefulness!" He cuffed Will hard enough to make him dizzy. Mistress Hornsby gave Father a glance of righteous approval but said nothing.

Only when they were safely inside the empty shop again did Father release him. He slammed the door. Then he turned to Will and demanded in a low voice, "What are you doing, boy? You should always hit them in the head first, don't you know? Never let them get you in the eye."

Will's mother sat on a stool and sobbed. "Now what has he done?" She leaned forward, with her skinny elbows on her knees, her face in her rough hands. In her lap she held a small crucifix. "Saint Winifred protect us!"

"Quiet, woman!" Father hissed. "Put that away."

Quickly she hid the forbidden crucifix in her pocket and stood up. "He's bleeding. Is he hurt?"

"He's fine," Father said in a brusque voice.

She reached up and gingerly touched Will's bruised temple. He winced. "I'm all right, Mother," he mumbled. Her anxious doting was more than he could bear. Across the cross passage in the house, he could hear his younger brothers' voices. He could hear his sister. Any moment they'd all be crowded into the shop asking questions, making him feel worse with their glad, cruel glances.

"William, William," Mother said, and shook her head. "Why must you disgrace us? You are supposed to set an example. Do you forget who you are, who you come from? Do you forget that my people—"

"Warwickshire's most distinguished family," Will grumbled, and stared at his feet. Why did she always have to bring up his lordly ancestors? The Ardens of Park Hall, who came in with William the Conqueror. The Ardens of Park Hall, who merited four long columns in the Domesday Book, the great record of properties in Great Britain. What good did being an Arden do him now?

"What cheek! Listen to your mother, young man!" Father barked, and smacked him in the back of the head.

"Yes, sir," Will said meekly. He took a deep breath to steel himself for what he knew was coming next. The unkindest cut of all.

"Look at me, William," Mother said. She trained her pale blue eyes on him like an expert archer with a drawn bow. "You had such promise. The very best scholar. Why must you fight and drink and disrespect your elders? You know you break my heart."

Will grimaced. "Forgive me, Mother."

"I pray to Saint Winifred for you every day, William," she continued. "I pray for your soul."

"Hush, now!" Father warned. He glanced nervously toward the open window. Anyone could have been listening. A neighbor, another of the church spies. Anyone. "Will," he whispered. "I heard about the fight. How it started. In jail they didn't make you say anything, did they? They didn't make you confess. You know what I mean, don't you?"

Will nodded slowly. "I didn't tell."

"Good boy," Father said. He seemed visibly relieved. "Wife, get some water for him. He's as filthy as a cesspit."

His mother made a quick sign of the cross and hurried out of the shop. Too exhausted to move, Will stared dully into space. His eyes scanned the shop's mostly empty shelves. The only objects for sale were a plain pair of workaday gloves of sheepskin with scroll stitching on the knuckles, two pair of men's kid leather gloves with plain cuffs, a fancy pair of buff-colored gauntlets embroidered with fruits and flowers, and one pair of ladies' wedding gloves, slightly used.

Painfully, Will pulled his arm from his doublet. He felt as if he'd been trampled by a hundred heavily loaded carts. From the inside of his clothing tumbled a piece of paper. It landed between his feet on the floor.

"What's this?" Father demanded. Before Will could stop him, he picked it up and unfolded it. Father stared hard at the writing.

Will gulped. "The little man with the bells. He gave it to me. Said to keep it safe."

"He did, did he? It appears to be a special letter admitting the presenter to the bailiff's performance."

"To hear the play!" Will said eagerly. He took the paper from his father and read. He forgot his bloody eye, his sore back, his bruised arms and legs. "This afternoon it says. I can go to the performance!"

"Are you mad?" Father hissed. "Don't think for a moment you can go. Wouldn't look right after I got you out of jail the way I did. Every alderman in the place will know about your mischief and wonder why you aren't locked up with the rest."

Will's mother shuffled into the shop with a pan of water and a rag. She placed them both on the stool and stood with her arms crossed in front of herself, staring at her whispering husband and son. "What foul deeds are you up to now?"

"Nothing, woman. Can't a man have some peace?" Father roared.

Mother, as usual, seemed unimpressed. "God is watching," she said, and left the room.

Will could not think of anything to say to Father, he was so filled with disappointment. It had been years since Will attended a performance at the guildhall.

Father plucked the paper from Will's fingers. "I'll go in your stead," he said. "We shouldn't waste the opportunity."

Will gritted his teeth. Father was the only other person who loved the theater as much as he did. It made perfect sense. Father would go and enjoy the performance by the great Alleyn. He'd see the spectacle in nine episodes, the great triumph of fighting. Meanwhile, Will would miss everything. As usual.

"There are other ways to see a play besides sitting in the hall," Father said, and winked.

Will felt confused. "Other ways?"

"I don't need to tell you, an expert scaler of trees," Father said in a low, confidential voice. "I don't need to tell you where the high window of the guildhall faces or how easy it is to perch among the leaves. I don't need to tell you."

A slow smile spread across Will's face. He knew exactly which tree—the elm that spread its branches beside the guildhall on the south side of the roof. A perfect perch. "How did you do it?" Will whispered.

"I don't climb trees anymore," Father replied in an indignant voice. "You can't accuse me."

"No, I mean, how did you convince them to set me free?"

"Helps to know the jailer. Past favors, you might say. Getting his son out of jail long ago—before the Great Misfortune." Father shrugged, then gave Will a crafty, sideways grin.

Chapter Four

Will pulled himself up inside the canopy of leaves and balanced on a fat limb. From his perch in the elm, he could watch the afternoon's performance through the top of the tall, open guildhall window. Will was too high to be noticed by passersby on the ground below and too concealed to alarm the audience seated indoors.

He had a perfect view of the crude raised platform that served as a stage at one end of the long hall. Scenery consisted of a leaning broom representing a tree and an overturned bucket for a chair. The stage was empty of actors. Will guessed that Alleyn and the others were probably out of sight pulling on their costumes.

The audience hummed with impatience. Restless aldermen squeezed side by side on wooden benches facing the platform. Will inspected the tops of heads and the crowns of hats. He recognized Father's balding pink scalp. Father had taken an inconspicuous place at the very back, as if to avoid drawing attention to himself.

Long, long ago, before the Great Misfortune, Father always sat right in the very front row. Will—just a young boy—stood between Father's rough knees and watched the players and puppeteers who came to beg the bailiff and the other aldermen for a license. Will felt thrilled and terrified at the same time, waiting breathlessly for the curtain to part.

Once, a huge face with a gaping, awful mouth breathed fire. Another time, sooty figures calling themselves Lost Souls danced around evil Herod, who was dressed in wild nightmare colors and flourished a long sword. Will hid his eyes when Devil and his tormenter, Vice, swaggered, raged, and shouted onstage. The sight gave him terrible dreams for weeks.

As Will grew older he memorized the miracle plays on Corpus Christi Day, the mummer's plays, and the jests from *The Hundred Merry Tales*. To Father's delight, Will could repeat every joke, every taunt of Beatrice and Benedick. He knew by heart the lines of Angel and Good and Evil. He made his mother laugh by acting out the pranks of Blessing,

Everyman, Charity, Folly, and Pleasure. For Will anything seemed possible onstage. Ghosts, fairies, and witches came alive and made terrible mischief. Valiant Saint George might be slain in combat but was always brought back to life by magic elixir.

Suddenly a trumpet flourished. The crowd became quiet. Onto the stage glided elegant Alleyn. He bowed and begged the aldermen's forgiveness for a last-minute change. "Because of some difficulties with ruined props and an unfortunate fray involving our only cart, we will be presenting *A Play of Love* by the great dramatist John Heywood in place of the spectacle in nine episodes advertised earlier." He exited without another word.

Will sighed with disappointment. He had looked forward to the battle scenes. A love story sounded insipid. And yet he felt compelled to stay. Sitting in a tree was much more enjoyable than going home and scraping hair from doeskins.

There were only four actors in the production. Alleyn played melancholy Lover Not Loved in crumpled disarray. The dwarf capered about as the mischievous vice No Lover, who wore bright colored hose and a spectacular hat stuffed with fireworks. A boy in woman's clothes took the part called Loved

Not Loving. And lastly, a foolishly cheerful actor performed as Lover Loved. As the story unfolded, each character seemed determined to prove that he or she was the most overwhelmed by emotion.

No Lover declared in a loud, sending voice:

The love that I owe you is original
Ground of my late joy and present pain all
And by this mean, love is ever more laid
between two angels, one good and one bad,
Hope and dread, which two be always at strife
Which one of them both with love shall rule most right.

Such grand words! Such earsplitting passion! How was such magic created, Will wondered. The short plays he had written long ago as amusements for his younger brothers and sister were never so musical and pleasing to the ear as Heywood's work. Will's simple productions, which had been staged using sheets hung from ropes tied between trees in the small orchard behind their house, always turned into disastrous affairs. Whenever Will tried to enliven his original plays with onstage murders and dramatic deaths, the cast of seven- and eight-year-olds would veer from his script and continue the fights nonstop. Someone always got hurt or stung by bees and ran home bleeding and crying. And that would be the end of the performance.

The Earl of Worcester's Men were a cut above all the other theatrical troupes Will had ever seen perform. Young Alleyn, so striking and magnetic, sawed the air with his hands and spoke as loud as fifty town criers. Even the dwarf, as No Lover, seemed to have leaped from his original skin. The audience roared with laughter at his bawdy motions, his rude dancing and mannerisms. Heywood's play seemed magical yet believable. Even with simple scenery the script made the setting convincing. And as for action—what sword fights, what lovemaking, what a marvelous exploding hat!

The lovers' plight spoke to Will with such directness, he wondered if Heywood had written the play especially for him. From the way the actors spoke and the audience laughed, Will began to wonder why true love, which sounded either unattainable or painful, should be so tirelessly sought.

When the performance ended, the crowd of aldermen applauded with vigor. Father's bullfrog cheer roared above the rest. Carefully Will lowered himself from the tree. He crept around the stone fence to make himself as invisible as possible, following his father's suggestion.

The chattering aldermen poured from the guildhall. From the sound of their satisfied chatter, it seemed they must have given their approval to the Earl of Worcester's Men.

Determined, Will slipped to the door near the stage area, the place he knew the actors always exited after they collected their license from the bailiff. Sure enough, the players exploded outdoors, still filled with a kind of windblown energy. Among the group he spotted Alleyn, who alone appeared neither noisy nor pleased.

Dare he speak to him and compliment his performance? Shyly Will took a step, then stopped, too tongue-tied to say anything. Although he and Alleyn were almost the same age, the actor seemed far more self-assured and worldly. Will racked his brain for a clever phrase. He adjusted and readjusted his cap.

Too late! Miserably he watched Alleyn disappear up the road with the other actors.

"Sir?" a voice said.

Will looked down, startled. The little man tugged at his sleeve. He had removed his costume as No Lover and now wore a sober, dark green velvet jerkin and bright yellow hose. He swept off his black felt hat and gazed up at Will with bulging eyes. Traces of caked whitish makeup clotted some of the stubble on his chin.

"So you came. Good," the little man said. He

reached up again, and this time gave Will a conciliatory pat on the elbow. It was as far as he could reach. "Thank you for helping me fight." His voice sounded proud, as if he believed he could easily have succeeded in the brawl single-handedly. "Physical prowess, stamina, combat skills with knife and dagger—these are all essential qualities for a player."

Will looked puzzled. He couldn't remember the little man throwing even one punch during the brawl.

The little man smiled and cocked his big head. He examined Will with a piercing, childish stare. "You enjoyed our performance?"

Will felt too embarrassed to admit he'd watched the performance from a tree. "Yes, sir, it was a true wonder."

"Can you sing?"

Will nodded, confused.

"Can you play an instrument? Perhaps the cittern, the bandore, the lute, or the bass viol?"

Will smiled. "I strum the lute, though some would say I am not expert."

"Can you dance?"

Will chuckled. "My dancing is passable, sir."

The little man looked him up and down. "You seem robust, well made, though your clothing is quite filthy. I suppose you own no velvets or silks of a gentleman. It is essential to wear clothes gracefully."

"Sir, what do you mean?"

"Stand up straight. Tuck in your chin," the little man commanded. "Hold your elbow thus, your hand thus. Good. Now, sir, what is your profession?"

"I am a . . . a glover's apprentice," Will admitted.

"An apprentice!" the little man exclaimed. "I took you for a gentleman of great living, for if by outward habit men should be judged, you would be taken for a substantial man."

Will grinned and made an elegant bow.

"Do you enjoy the work?"

"As a gentleman," Will said, using Sir Lucy's proud voice, "I do not work."

The little man chuckled. "Excellent response. Now for the truth. Do you enjoy working as a glover?"

Will took a deep breath. He didn't know how to answer. The question wasn't something he'd ever before considered. A person worked because he must, not because he enjoyed it.

The little man impatiently wrinkled his nose. "You should do what gives you passion."

"What gives me passion?" Will said nervously. *Perhaps the fellow's bewitched.*

"How's your memory?" the little man persisted.

Will's eyes darted to the left, to the right. This odd

fellow didn't look dangerous, but then again he might have some power.

"For such a strong, healthy young man, you seem sometimes short on wit." The little man tapped the toe of his long shoe. "When I speak of memory, I mean, can you hear a speech and say it back?"

"Some have said as much," Will replied slowly. He had no idea where this new line of questioning was going. "The schoolmaster bade us give speeches often enough."

"Let's see then. Pray, repeat a speech from the performance."

Will blushed, wishing his claim did not have so much bragging in it. "Which speech?"

"Any one you like."

"I'll speak yours, the one you gave to Lover Loved." Will cleared his throat and began:

"No lover? No, by God I warrant you
I am no lover in such manner meant as doth appear in
*   the purpose present.*
For as touching women, go where I shall
I am at one point with women all:
The smoothest, the smirkiest, the smallest,
The truest, the trimmest, the tallest,
The wisest, the wiliest, the wildest,

The merriest, the mannerliest, the mildest,
The strangest, the straightest, the strongest,
The lusterest, the lest, or the longest,
The rashest, the ruddiest, the roundest,
The sagest, the sallowest, the soundest,
The coyest, the curstest, the coldest,
The busiest, the brightest, the boldest,
The thankfulest, the thinnest, the thickest,
The saintliest—"

"That's enough, anon," interrupted the little man, a bit flustered. "You spoke it well for a beginner."

"Thank you, sir."

"Have you ever traveled?"

"Only as far as Snitterfield."

The little man made a *tsk-tsk* noise behind his teeth. "So you've never been to London?"

"No, sir."

The little man sighed. "Home-keeping youths have ever homely wits," he said under his breath. Leaning forward, he said in a most confidential voice, "You know the theater is a worthy profession."

Will didn't know how to reply. What was this fellow talking about? Actors were masterless men who practiced an art most people despised. Churchmen called it devil's work. Town officials tolerated players with proper papers only a little better than vagabonds and beggars. After a performance or two, aldermen chased theater companies out of town as quickly as possible. Any actor who lingered in a town overlong—without job or home—could be arrested, put in the stocks, and branded.

"As I said before," the little man continued, "you should do what gives you passion."

The skin on the back of Will's neck prickled with suspicion. *Surely he's making fun of me.* Besides, who did anything for a passion? A man's role in life was pre-ordained. The son of a baker became a baker. The son of a glover became a glover. This little man was obviously confused or crazy.

And yet . . .

There seemed something exhilarating, even astounding, in what the little man had suggested.

"Think about what I have told you." The little man waved farewell. He swept his hat back on his large head and strutted up Chapel Street.

Will watched him go. He sucked in and bit his lower lip. He should hurry home and hide before he was questioned about how he got out of jail. And yet he could not move.

"A worthy profession." What if he ran away, joined the theater company, and one day became as famous

as Alleyn? And why not? He was just as strong and fit and young and willing to work hard. He had a good memory. He could fight. He could sing. He could improvise the part of a gentleman. Perhaps he could write. What if he were able to create plays as good as Heywood's? Of course, there'd be plenty of action, spectacle, and great triumph of—

"Will, get home!"

Will jumped at the sound of Father's shrill command coming from around the corner of the guild-hall. In a panic Will darted down the street back toward the shop.

As Will loped along he knew he'd never leave. Never. He'd be trapped here forever.

Chapter Five

Time passed, and soon July meadows rioted with yellow buttercups, the sweep of white marguerites, and purple clover. Bees buzzed. Grain ripened. The pace of work quickened in the fields outside town held in common by the farmers.

Diving swallows hungrily followed a line of men who advanced like the edge of a wave through the full growth of hissing grass. Scythe blades flashed. Fat grasshoppers leaped. Birds feasted. Under the hot sun the fields swarmed with pockets of redolent odor—the sweet, rich scent of newly cut hay. A warm wind blew west and the fields' perfume floated into town.

For weeks after the departure of the Earl of Worcester's Men, Will felt more restless than ever. He tried not to think about what the little man had told him. *Nothing but nonsense.* Instead, he devoted all his energy to his work. He did his best to avoid drunken brawls, disrespect, and other mischief that might involve churchmen, constables, or jail. It wasn't long, however, before his resolve began to waver.

Maybe it was the smell of hay. Maybe it was the heat. Maybe it was the boredom. Maybe it was the full moon. Whatever the reason, one night after downing numerous tankards at Attwood's, Will came up with a brilliant idea. Accompanied by his friend Richard Field, home for a few days from his apprenticeship in London, he would creep under cover of darkness into the forbidden woods at Charlecote.

The plan was risky, foolish, and absolutely enticing to Will, who only felt truly alive when he was in the most danger. And he could not have selected a more perilous place in which to trespass. Charlecote contained Sir Lucy's special park of trees and open meadow, where rabbits ran free for royal hunting parties. No one from town was allowed to enter the property, bordered by the river and a tall fence made of sharp pikes. Poaching was punishable by steep fines and imprisonment.

And yet neither the river, the barricade, nor the law dissuaded Will and Richard, who carried a borrowed bow and a quiver of arrows. The two young men tramped up the muddy riverbank toward the forest. They had been friends forever.

"A race?" Will said as soon as they reached the edge of the game preserve.

"In the dark?" Richard replied without much enthusiasm.

"Come, man! Moon's bright enough to read your palm," Will said, and hiccuped. "You've been in the city too long. You know the place where the stream cuts across the path. Look lively." Will took off at full speed.

Branches whipped past Will's face. Briars snagged his jerkin, gouged his legs, and tore his sleeves, but he was too drunk to feel any pain. He scrambled over slick fallen logs, plunged into gullies, and clambered up muddy hills. No one could stop him. Not even Sir Lucy's game warden. The pure joy of movement, the exhilaration of danger—these were the only things that mattered. He felt invincible, free.

Moonlight bewitched the woods. Fantastic gibbous shapes shook and stuttered in the wind. Slants of moonbeam through leaves seemed to set whole bushes afire with strange moon glows and glints.

In a landscape altered so profoundly by such strange light, anything was possible. Will should have known this as soon as he passed the purlieu, the game preserve boundary. He should have recognized the warning signs—the fusty odor of wormwood, the faint burning scent of brimstone, the hooting of an owl. Only when he rounded a copse of trees was he aware of a low sound like a cry of pain.

He slowed. His heart slammed against his ribs. And for the first time he was aware of sweat pouring down his forehead and trickling down the inside of his arms.

Oooo-la-la-ooooooooo-la.

"Who's there?" he called, suddenly sober. He strained to make out a shape. The shadows took on a life form: jerk of elbow, crook of knee, twist of head. The breeze rattled the leaves and confused the eye.

Oooo-la-la-ooooooooo-la.

Will gulped. The sound did not seem human. Without thinking, he made the sign of the cross over and over again, hoping against hope that what lurked ahead was not what he feared most.

He peered into the clearing. Something solid moved. The shape, dark and bent like an old cedar, hobbled across the small open space and paused, as if listening.

This was no tree. This, Will knew, was a witch.

Not daring to breathe, he managed to slip silently behind the nearest pine. He pressed his cheek hard against the sticky bark. If he moved a muscle, if he blinked, if he inhaled even the smallest breath, she would know. And just like every angry witch he'd ever heard about, she would cast a curse on him.

He shut his eyes tight and waited. Will had heard how hags' human victims lost their wits with hysteria, grimaced like apes, and tumbled like hedgehogs. They muttered words of owl-blasted gibberish like "*Obus, bobus,*" then, *poof,* turned into slouching dogs and later sickened and died.

If he ran, she would find him. If he stayed, she would find him. Escape seemed impossible.

"Do not be stricken with fear," a withered voice said. The words seemed to be part wind, part leaf, part moonlight.

Will felt his legs turn to stone.

"How perilous is it," the voice asked, "to choose not to love the life we're shown?"

Will peeled his cheek from the bark of the tree and bravely peeked around. In the puddle of moonlight, the black shape looked even blacker. He could recognize no eyes, no mouth, no nose—only the outline of a shape that seemed no bigger than the dwarf from the Earl of Worcester's Men.

"Thy fate, dost thou wish to know it?" she called.

The wind buffeted the tree. Something finally shook Will free. He had to escape.

He took off at a wild gallop, heading back the way he had come. He lurched over fallen logs and dodged bushes. He couldn't be sure, but behind him he thought he heard the high sound of laughter. In all his life he never ran so hard, so fast, so long. He struggled with each step. His legs plunged knee-deep in mud. His clothing caught on brambles. He twisted and thrashed through razor-sharp thorns.

Breathless, bleeding, he stumbled toward what he hoped was the river—the edge of Charlecote.

"Will!"

Exhausted, Will pumped his knees slower, slower. He leaned forward, clutched his thighs with both hands, and gulped for air—aware of a rotting odor that reminded him of an old cellar.

"Will!" The hulking figure of Richard crashed through the bushes. "You're a tenderhearted one! Where did they go?"

"What?" Will asked. "How many did you see?" He and Richard had to flee before it was too late.

"Let's go back and take a shot."

Horrified, Will grabbed his friend's arm. "Arrows are powerless."

"What? We can't have come all this way for nothing."

"Dangerous business," Will whispered in an urgent voice. "Get out while we can."

Richard refused to budge. "What *kind* of rabbits does Sir Lucy breed here? They must be monstrous."

"Rabbits?" said Will slowly. "You're talking about rabbits?"

"Something's wrong with you. Some dotage's taken over your brain, Will. We came here to shoot coneys, remember? I haven't seen a single one. Then you come racing along scared to death."

"I'm not scared," insisted Will, still shaking.

"Don't you remember the wager? At Attwood's we agreed to hunt coneys. Then you shout about a race to the stream and run off like some wild hart with falling sickness, leaving me to follow you best I can." With much huffing and puffing, Richard collapsed onto the ground. "Have a drink, Will."

Will grabbed the leather bottle and gulped. The liquor burned his throat. He was still alive! He felt his legs, his arms. He hadn't been turned into a frog or a bat.

"You sick? You seem so strange."

"I'm fine," Will said in a quavering voice. He sat hunched on the ground. What if she's listening? Had he really seen that shape and heard that voice?

Maybe it was just Robin Goodfellow playing tricks on him.

Richard grabbed the bottle from his friend. Will was glad it was too dark for Richard to see how his hand shook. "A fat, greasy rabbit cooked on a spit," Richard grumbled. "That's what you promised."

"Did I?" Will glanced over his shoulder. The forest seemed to have eyes. Again he heard that strange voice. *"How perilous is it to choose not to love the life we're shown?"*

Richard belched. "How we supposed to shoot a rabbit in the dark?"

Something slithered and rustled among the leaves.

" 'A little poaching,' you says, 'for old times' sake.' Course if we get caught by Sir Lucy's men," Richard complained, "we'll go to prison for one month."

"Three months."

"Oh, now that makes me feel a great deal better, thank you very much," Richard said with disgust. "Lose my apprenticeship in the city. Anne'll never have me."

Will groaned. "Not Anne again."

"You've got to help me, Will." Richard's voice sounded broken, as if he might burst into sobs at any moment. "You've got to write the sonnet. I haven't much time to make her change her mind."

Will felt disgusted hearing his friend blubber.

What did Richard have to feel so sorry for himself about? He was the only one from their school who ever successfully fled their small, backward town. Richard had all the luck, all the talent. He was working for a promising printer in London—the real city, the place where life had possibilities. "Give me the bottle," Will grumbled, and took a long swig.

"I need a sonnet. You're my only hope."

"Why not just copy one?"

"She'll know. She's learned. Not like the drabs, giglots, and wenches you favor. She reads and appreciates real literature." Richard paused and took a swig. "I need an original. Something ravishingly good. Good enough to convince her to love me."

Will sucked in his breath. He'd let pass the comment about drabs, giglots, and wenches—at least for the time being. "You sound as stupid as a mooncalf—"

A hound howled in the distance. They both froze.

"Sir Lucy's men," Will said between clenched teeth.

"What?"

"Run!"

Chapter Six

"Follow me to the river!" Will shouted.

Richard grabbed the quiver of arrows and the bow. Together they scrambled through briars, over fallen trees, past clinging vines. Will wasn't sure if they were even going in the right direction. He only knew that if they could somehow make it to the river, dive in, and swim, the dog might lose their scent and they could escape.

"Saints preserve us! Saints preserve us!" Richard mumbled as he trotted behind Will.

The racket! "Can you move faster?" Will called. "Or quieter?"

Richard only grunted and lumbered along with the stealth of an oxcart. *We'll never make it out of here.* For the first time, Will sensed what it must be like to be a rabbit racing and coursing away from the hounds.

The hound bayed again, closer now.

The two friends rounded the bend of some part of the woods that looked distinctly unfamiliar to Will. Had the moonlight confused him? *Lost!* He was sure of it now. No matter how hard he pushed himself through the undergrowth, he didn't seem to make any progress. *A nightmare.*

"They're nearly on us!" Richard said in a shrill voice.

Will considered climbing a tree. He could turn himself in. He could throw himself upon the mercies of Sir Lucy. But his father would never be able to save him from jail a second time. Rioting and brawling and now trespassing and poaching. He'd be trapped forever in that dank prison cell. "Run faster!" Will called to Richard. The dog yowled louder, louder yet.

"Can't go on," Richard groaned. He floundered to a dead stop, breathing hard and smelling of cheese and sack and sweat. Will wanted to kick him hard— like a donkey—to make him go. "Escape without me," Richard whispered.

"No," Will replied. Then he added in his most convincing voice, "The river's just a little farther. We'll be safe soon." He clutched Richard's thick arm and tugged. "Think of Anne. Think of your future."

Richard lumbered forward, slow at first and then

faster. Will grabbed the bow and the arrows, uncertain where he and Richard were, no idea where they were going.

The hound bayed again.

Will's feet throbbed. His legs ached. He licked his lip and tasted the metallic flavor of blood. He must have cut his face. Desperately, he trotted faster, bow and arrows under his arm. He regretted every sin he had ever committed. He prayed to God that if he managed to escape from this predicament, he would change his ways. Every Sunday he'd go to church. He'd stay sober. He'd stay away from Mopsa. He wouldn't fight, cheat, or lie ever again. He'd work hard and finish his apprenticeship and make his family proud of him. He'd do anything. *Please, God, just let me outrun this dog.* "Make haste, Richard!"

In a clearing, they nearly ran headlong into what seemed to be a fence or a hedge. Will paused. Something about this place. What was it? He'd been here before—unless the moonlight was playing tricks again. "Look!" Will said eagerly.

Richard wheezed and gasped for breath. He could barely speak. "What?"

"A house," Will said triumphantly. "A house I know!"

"Sweet Jesus preserve us!"

The sound of the dog and the shouting of men grew louder, more distinct. The two friends had only a few moments—a few seconds—before they'd be discovered and captured. "Burst of speed!" Will said. He dashed across the clearing with Richard at his heels. No light shone from within the small thatched cottage. Will ran around behind the house and rapped on the shutter covering the back window.

"Who goes there?" a sleepy voice called.

"Uncle!" Will whispered. "It's me. Will."

"Trouble again?"

"What else?"

The shutter opened. By some great stroke of luck and superhuman strength, Will—still clutching the bow and arrows—managed to hoist himself inside the cottage window headfirst. Then he and his uncle hauled the bulky body of Richard to safety.

"Over there!" Hal hissed. "You know the place."

The dog yowled so clearly, it sounded as if it were already in the clearing. Will jabbed Richard and motioned for him to follow him as he scuttled across the cottage's rush-strewn dirt floor to a wooden table. Like a madman, Will shoved aside the table and scooped up the rushes.

"Get under, man!" Will whispered.

"A table won't hide us both. We're too big."
Richard sounded as if he might begin to cry.

"Not the table. The trapdoor. Hurry!"

Pounding shook the front door. "Let us in!"
someone shouted. The dog yelped and scratched.

Will tugged on a small iron ring. The trapdoor in
the floor opened. Will threw the bow and arrows down
into the small, dark cellar, then jumped in after them.

"Open up!"

"A moment anon!" Hal bellowed. He gave
Richard a good shove down into the cellar. "Tell me
all about it later," he whispered with an irritating
sense of delight. Then he quietly shut the trapdoor.

Will and Richard crouched in the small space
below the floor, surrounded by the odor of rotten
cabbage and mice droppings. Curled like potato
bugs, they could neither sit up nor move. There was
no room to spare. Overhead the table legs scraped
against the trapdoor. Rushes rustled and scratched as
they were replaced over the hiding place.

"What if he tells?" Richard whispered.

Will budged his elbow enough to give Richard a
poke in the ribs. Will was certain he could trust
Uncle Hal. Uncle Hal knew what it felt like to be in
trouble with the law. In the past twenty-odd years

he'd been arrested for trespassing, debt, failure to mend the Queen's Highway, and wearing a hat instead of a woolen cap to church—the required Sunday headgear. He'd been called into court for not paying his taxes, for fighting, and for slander. Uncle Hal, known in town as a wag and a scoundrel, didn't seem to care what other people thought. "Nothing like a bloody fray," he always said, "to keep a man's humors in order."

Time crawled. Will felt sure that the whole cottage must be echoing with the sound of Richard's labored breathing. Something slithered and scritched overhead. Then heavy footsteps. Muffled voices. His uncle's ingratiating, flattering bass. *Good*. And now the insistent tenor of Sir Lucy's men. More flattering bass. More tenor. Outside came the frantic soprano howling of the dog. The creature sounded as if it were throwing itself against the cottage wall.

"And good night to you both," Hal said in a voice both clear and bright. *Clunk!* Perhaps a door shutting overhead.

Something rattled. The trapdoor opened. Hal's bright pink, fleshy face beamed down at them from beneath his sleeping cap. He held aloft a candle. With his free hand he motioned for Will and Richard to crawl up.

"Haven't changed a bit, Will, have you?" said Hal,

winking. "And you, Richard, this would be a bit of disarray for you if you was caught, aye?"

Richard stiffly hoisted himself out of the trap-door. He crawled in a humiliating fashion across the room and sat on the floor, slumped against the wall. He refused to sit in a chair because he claimed that someone would spy him through an open window.

"You're sure they're gone, Uncle?" Will asked in a low voice. His knees shook and his sweat-soaked shirt stuck to his back.

"They'll not be back," Hal replied. "I told them I saw their wives at the Angel earlier this evening and did they know they were out so late?"

Father was right. Uncle Hal had a conscience that stretched as easily as cheverel, the most supple kid-skin. Hal would say anything to anyone to make sure he got what he wanted.

"A drink, Will?" Uncle Hal asked.

Will nodded wearily, immediately forgetting his vow of sobriety. He licked his lips as his uncle uncorked a bottle of sack.

"Tell all, sirrah," Hal said eagerly, and straddled a chair. He handed Will the leather bottle. "Poaching rabbits again? What I would give for a chance to have been with you. Catch anything? A snare's good, but of course, there are those that prefer a bow. Don't forget your weapon in my cellar, now. I've a mind to proportion anything what comes to my place and doesn't have legs. God's eyes, it's a good thing you found me before they found you! Those game wardens were full of fury, that's for sure. And that dog was blood-mad. Had to explain that the reason the mongrel was so conglomerated was on account of the pig I slaughtered, which was a base lie."

Will was unable to get a word in edgewise. He didn't care. He was too tired to speak. Instead, he took a long sip. Then he wiped his mouth with the back of his bloodied hand. He glanced over at Richard, who snored, mouth open, head back against the wall. He looked like a gaping, doomed fish hanging from a hook out of water.

Chapter Seven

The next morning a raucous flock of crows roosted in the elms outside Will's bedroom window. Below on Henley Street children shouted and screamed insults. Wagons rumbled along the dirt road. Oxen bawled. Drivers bellowed. And up and down the way, the peddlers howled their morning songs:

> *"Come pretty maidens, what is't you buy?*
> *See what is't you lack?*
> *If you can find a toy to your mind,*
> *Be so kind, view the peddler's pack."*

Will opened his eyes slowly, painfully. Why was it that every single one of the 1,567 souls in town must torture him awake today? He rolled over, with a musty blanket shielding his face. He squeezed his eyes shut. His head throbbed. No matter how hard he tried, he could not shake his nightmare—the vision of a dark hag in the woods calling to him: *"Thy fate, dost thou wish to know it?"*

Everything that had happened last night seemed as strange and impossible as the hag's voice, her words. Were they really running through the woods chased by the game warden's hound? Did they hide in Uncle Hal's cellar? Even now, Will had no idea how he and Richard had made it home. He rubbed his sore jaw. The inside of his mouth tasted as dry as old chicken skin and as foul as a slaked lime pit—the usual effect, he knew, of Uncle Hal's favorite drink, sack.

"Awake! William, arise!" Mother shouted up the stairs from the hall. "You'll be late for work again."

Will groaned and pulled the blanket from his face. He lifted himself from the pallet on the floor as feebly as a stiff old man. His brothers' beds were empty. Through the floorboards he could hear two-year-old Edmond mewling unmercifully.

He pulled on his breeches and climbed down the steps to the hall, where a fire burned. The smell of burning wood and glutinous beans bubbling in a pot over the fire gave Will a queasy feeling in his stomach. "Something to eat?" Mother said, and gave the pot a stir.

"No, madame," Will replied. He avoided getting

too close to Edmond, who had smeared his snotty face with his breakfast. Pesky eight-year-old Richard and Gilbert, sixteen, shoveled gray, gooey frumenty from a shared wooden trencher into their smacking mouths.

Richard smiled as soon as he saw Will. "There was a madman had five sons. Pickle Herring, Blue Breeches, Pepper Breeches—and what's the other one you said?"

"I wish I was deaf," Will said miserably. He snagged a piece of Gilbert's bread and took a small nibble. "Must you speak so terribly loud every morning? His name was Ginger Breeches."

"That's not enough brothers," said Gilbert. "You got only four."

Richard's lip trembled. "Will, tell him I am trying to tell your story. He is making me forget."

"It's not my story," Will said, and groaned. He closed his eyes and rubbed his temples. "It's the Mummer's play. The other brother was Allspice."

"Allspice, he's the one I remembered! See, all the sons kill their father with swords. Like this." Richard poked his littlest brother hard with a wooden spoon, so that he began to scream again.

"Merciful heavens!" Mother scolded. "Will, can you not keep your brothers from committing violence? I turn my back for one minute and—"

"I'm leaving," Will said, holding his hands over his ears.

"Pickle Herring!" Richard shouted over Edmond's wails. "Pickle Herring!"

"Can't you do anything right, Will?" Mother picked up the sticky, shrieking baby. "Everything was perfectly peaceful before you walked in here."

"Pickle Herring stamps his foot and then his father comes back to life," Richard announced. "Isn't that right, Will?"

Will retreated toward the door. "I'm off to work. Tell me later, Richard."

"Wait! Wait, Will," Richard called in anguish. "You can't leave yet. I didn't tell about fighting the Wild Worm!"

Richard's piercing voice echoed in Will's ears as he stumbled out to the garden privy, commonly called the jakes. It was a wooden seat with a hole cut in it and a cesspit beneath. This warm morning the jakes smelled especially pungent. Will brushed away the buzzing black flies and slowly made his way to the shop next door. Like the other buildings on Henley Street, the house and shop were half-timbered buildings made of oak beams and thatched with straw. A cross-passage connected the house to the shop.

Today the shop was filled with the sharp odor of alum and salt from newly cured hides hanging from the ceiling. The smell made Will feel as if he might vomit. He should not have eaten that bread. He looked around the shop and noticed Joan. Now his stomach felt even worse.

Joan stopped scribbling with quill and paper and studied her eldest brother. "You look accursed. In a fight again?"

Will took a deep breath. "No. Leave me alone." He hoped there'd be no customers for a while and he could sleep out of sight on the pile of hides behind the counter. Perhaps Joan would keep watch for Father.

While Joan went back to her scribbling, Will slunk behind the counter and carefully lowered his head onto the crook of his elbow. He shut his eyes.

"Where," Joan demanded in a strident voice, "were you last night after the last curfew bell tolled?"

Will pretended to be asleep.

"Why playact that you cannot hear?" She kept scribbling. He could hear the *scritch-scratch-scritch* and wondered why she persisted in this unwomanly habit. There was nothing attractive about a girl who knew how to write. Sending her to the free school had been their father's idea. Joan was only supposed to learn to read the Bible. Learning to write was something she managed to acquire by eavesdropping on the lessons for Will and the other boys. Joan was an excellent eavesdropper. That was another reason Will tried to talk as little as possible in front of his sister. "Where were you?" she demanded again, even louder.

"Home abed," Will said in a dull voice. "Can you be quiet for once?"

"Home abed? Ha!" she exclaimed. "Is that how your boots became so muddy and your face so scratched?"

Will stretched out one sore leg, opened one eye, and inspected his foot. He had forgotten to scrape his boots clean. That was a minor matter. But his face—now that was important. Slowly he sat up. He hadn't even looked in the glass yet this morning. What if someone came into the shop and noticed his disarray?

As casually as he could, he stood and sauntered to the cracked glass hanging from a peg on the wall. He peered at his reflection in horror. His cheeks were scraped, filthy. He had a nasty cut over his eyebrow, and his dark hair stood straight up. He licked his hand and tried to rub away the dirt. As best he could, he ran his fingers through his unruly, curly hair.

He looked at himself again in the mirror, this time a sideways view. It amazed him how girls always remarked upon his hair. No one ever made much of his appearance until last year, when he shot up about two inches in less than a season. Before he had always been small, thin, and mouseish. He cocked his head to one side and lifted one eyebrow, like the foppish gentleman he had demonstrated for the little man.

Joan made a loud clucking sound. "Aren't you the great preening peacock!"

Will quickly glanced away from the glass. He pretended to be inspecting a pair of new gloves.

"Father's going to be angry you were late again."

"Father's always angry," Will replied bitterly. "Is it my fault that wool brogging went bad? Is it my fault that Mother's precious land had to be sold off?"

"Be quiet!" Joan hissed. No one in the family was allowed to speak of Father's illegal wool trading business or the constant preying of debt collectors. "What's wrong with you?"

"Nothing." Will's eyes darted toward the window, wondering how quickly Father might return.

"You should be more careful. You nearly knocked the shutter off when you climbed inside last night. It's hanging by one latch now."

Will tried to find a comfortable spot behind the counter again. "The wind did it."

Joan sniffed. "O Brother dearest, you lie."

"O Sister dearest, that your face were not so full of *O's!*"

Joan remained eerily silent. Now it was Will's turn to feel triumphant. He knew his sister did not like to be reminded of her smallpox scars, the pitted circles on her face.

Now, perhaps, she'll leave me alone. He shut his eyes and again tried to get some well-needed sleep. In spite of all his effort, he tossed and turned. "Joan?"

No answer.

"Joan, I am sorry for what I said."

Joan cleared her throat. "Apology accepted. It will not kill you, I hope, to hear my new poem."

Will moaned. "All right, then. Only not too loud."

Joan read from her paper:

*"From you have I been absent in the spring,
When proud-pied April, dressed in all his trim,
Hath put a spirit of youth in everything . . ."*

She paused. "What do you think so far?"

"Keep going," Will said. He hoped he sounded encouraging, even though he could not understand why Joan fancied herself a poet. When winter came and Joan turned fourteen, Mother said she'd be ready to go away from home and begin work as a servant. Being a poet was a very lamentable idea for a girl whose only prospects were to clean and cook for some lazy yeoman's wife.

"That heavy Saturn laughed and leaped with him;
Yet nor the lays of birds, nor the sweet smell
Of different flowers in odor and in hue,
Could make me any summer's story tell . . ."

Will took a great breath of air, then let it out all at once. "What means *proud-pied* and *lays of birds?*"

" 'Decorated' and 'birds' nests.' I don't know. I had to make it rhyme!" Joan wailed. She scratched furiously with her pen. "I'll blot the line. It is imperfect. Like everything else I do."

Will could tell from the tremble in her voice she was about to cry. Any moment she would burst into tears. He couldn't stand it when she cried. "It's not bad," he said hurriedly. "I've heard worse. And the part about . . . about heavy Saturn. That was interesting."

"Fie!" She ripped the paper into tiny pieces. "It's foul stuff!"

Will sat up and hugged his knees. He felt sick to his stomach. "A love poem is it?" he said cheerfully. "I think it has some possibility." Talking only made his head throb more. "Who's it for?"

"None of your business," she mumbled. She wiped her inky fingers on a rag.

Will sighed. There was no use trying to talk to her when she was in one of her foul moods. He rested again on the skins.

Joan picked up the broom and swept the floor with noisy abandon. "When does Richard go back to London?"

"Today," Will said. Again he recalled last night. He massaged his temples slowly. This, too, did no good.

"Will you be seeing him before he goes?"

Her sudden recovery and the sweetness in her voice made Will suspicious. "He is almost twenty-two years old, and you are only thirteen," he said sternly. "There's eight years' difference between you."

Joan stopped sweeping and looked at him coyly. "What does that matter when love's involved?"

Will groaned. His sister was a fool! Richard had paid as much attention to her as to a bent groat.

"One day," Joan persisted in a dreamy voice, "Richard's going to ask for my hand in marriage. I know he loves me. He just doesn't realize it yet. I have had a sign."

"From a cuckoo bird?" Will growled.

"No, from a fortune-teller. She said if I were as much beloved, perhaps I should not be so much in love."

Will snorted. "Now, there's pretty advice! I hope you did not pay too much for that information."

Joan began sweeping again. "Of course, there's the matter of where we'll live."

"Of course." Will yawned and closed his eyes. He'd wait to tell her about Richard and his wooing of Anne. No use destroying her childish fantasy right now. After all, her murmuring chatter about her future happiness was lulling him to sleep.

"London is not the most healthful climate to raise a family," Joan continued. "So I think that a house in the country and a house in town would be the best solution. I will require many beautiful dresses. Some to wear in town. Some for the country. I have them all sketched out. And, of course, good servants may be hard to find, but our children will benefit from a superior education and—are you listening?"

"Of course," Will said in a muffled voice.

"I will tell you the names I have chosen for our children. Are you listening? I will call them—"

Suddenly the draper's wife burst into the shop and slammed the door behind herself. Instinctively, Will rolled over onto his hands and knees and crawled into the deepest shadow behind the counter, where he hoped she wouldn't notice him.

"Good morning, Mistress Price," Joan said.

Biddy Price never bothered with trivial greetings when there was gossip to report. "Where's your father?" she demanded, out of breath.

"Out," said Joan. "I can tell him what you want him to know."

Biddy Price looked at Joan carefully, as if she wasn't sure she could trust her. But the news was about to burst from her mouth. She licked her pale lips. "Did you hear the penance?"

"Who's it this time?" Joan asked wearily.

"You're not too young to know. It might scare you into good behavior, girl," said Biddy in a confidential tone. "You remember William Burman of Shottery, who committed adultery with Margery, the wife of John Pyner, and then with Widow Attwood?"

Joan shrugged with little enthusiasm.

Biddy Price took a deep breath. "Now his brother Thomas made a clean breast of getting Susanna Ainge of Bridge Street with child. He's going to have to do penance two Sundays: confess the sin in detail, stand on a stool in the middle aisle near the pulpit covered in a white sheet head to foot, bareheaded, barefoot, and holding a white rod. Will you be there?" Biddy narrowed her eyes and sniffed as if she sensed the body of a dead rat somewhere in the shop.

"Oh, most certainly," Joan said. "Would you like to see some new gloves?"

"I say Thomas should have to do better than that," Biddy continued in a peevish voice. "He's going to have to pay something to the poor as well. That's what I heard." She shook her head in disgust. "We lives in times of outrageous seas of adultery, whoredom, fornication, and uncleanness."

"Yes, yes, Mistress. I'm afraid you're quite right. How about these sheepskin gloves? Are they not fine?"

"In the old days church court thought nothing of flogging such disrupters of society naked with a birch rod," Biddy said with so much vehemence, spit flew from her toothless mouth. "But now some among us count it no sin at all but rather a pastime, a dalliance, not to be rebuked but winked at."

"You don't say?"

"Speaking of dalliance," Biddy said, her gray eyes narrowing, "where's that brother of yours?"

"Which brother? I have four, madame." Joan seemed to struggle to muster a polite smile.

"The oldest, of course. The one who's a dawcock.

He should be warned. He's headed straight for hell if he's not careful."

"I'm sure he'd be grateful for your concern," said Joan. "Perhaps he'll thank you himself, if I can convince him to stop hiding from you."

"Hiding?" said Biddy with surprise. "Where?"

"Behind the counter," Joan replied.

"Good morning, Mistress." Sheepishly, Will stood up and made a little bow.

"You was lurking, weren't you? What rudeness!" exploded Biddy. The heavyset woman turned and stormed out of the shop. As she pushed through the door she nearly knocked over Father. He lifted the rim of his hat in greeting. Biddy pushed him aside and marched in a fury down Henley Street.

"Pray, what was all that about?" Father demanded.

"Will insulted Biddy Price, who only wanted to tell us the latest excommunication," Joan said in her Most Dutiful Daughter voice.

Will cowered behind the counter, filled with dread.

"Rebellious untowardliness!" Father shouted. "Your overmounting spirit is a curse!" His cheeks flushed the same mottled crimson as his bright nose. "We need customers, Will." He ran his hands through the white tufts of hair remaining on the sides of his head. "Was the cursed woman going to buy something?"

"Indeed I think so," Joan said.

Will groaned. Father always believed Joan. She had always been his favorite. "Biddy Price never buys anything, Father," Will protested. "She only comes to gossip."

"Have respect for your elders, you upstart!" Father shouted, louder this time. "Your rudeness makes a mockery of our family, our business, our good name . . ."

Will had heard this speech so many times, he didn't bother to listen anymore. He didn't dare argue with Father. What was the point? *Old pantaloon!* Will drummed the counter with his fingers.

Suddenly someone pounded on the door. The hard, precise knocking meant only one thing. Like a ghost, Father slunk to the doorway that led to the narrow stairway to the chamber over the shop. Father silently signaled to Joan.

Obediently, she tiptoed to the window and peeked outside. She mouthed silently the word "constable."

His face drained of all color, Father scurried out of sight. Will gulped. In a flash he, too, ducked up the stairway.

Chapter Eight

Father and son skulked breathlessly on the dusty stairs and listened to the voices in the room below.

"My father's not home, sir," Joan said.

"I'm not here again to try and collect fines or taxes," said the constable. "I'm here about your brother."

Will's heart leaped into his mouth. *More disgrace.* He couldn't bear to look at Father.

"Where was Will last night?" the constable demanded.

"Why do you ask, sir?"

There was a long pause, as if the dull-witted constable sensed he'd ruined his chance to find the evidence he needed. "We have a report from the game warden that two young men were poaching at Charlecote. Do you know anything about this?"

"No, Constable, sir, my brother was home last night."

"He wasn't out trespassing on Sir Lucy's hunting grounds?"

"No, sir, I can vouch for his whereabouts. He was in his bed snoring very loud."

Will felt a sudden sense of relief and gratitude. He and Father lingered upstairs until they heard the constable leave and the door close. They waited until Joan gave the all-clear signal by rapping three times on the ceiling with the end of the broom handle.

Will and Father shuffled down the stairs. "Well done, as usual, Daughter!" Father said. Will shot Joan an approving glance.

"I've had enough practice all these years," she replied with a wry smile that Father did not seem to notice.

Father turned to Will. "I hope that you have not been up near Snitterfield again with my brother. Uncle Hal is a bad influence. I've told you before. Stay away from him."

"Uncle Hal wasn't involved in anything illegal," Will insisted.

Father rocked back on his heels and pressed his fingers together as if he were a bishop. "Don't think I can bribe the jail keeper so easily a second time."

"Jail keeper?" Joan said with interest.

"You're a good girl," Father said. "It's nothing that you need to know about."

Will rolled his eyes. *That* was all his sister needed to hear. She'd be sure now to ferret out every detail of his time in the town jail.

From the house came the squalling of Edmond and the unmistakable voice of their mother. "Husband!"

"I've gone to Attwood's," Father said quickly. He slipped out the door and vanished down Henley Street.

"I owe you a favor," Will said.

Joan grinned. "That you do."

"What will it be?" Will asked, suspicious of her enthusiasm.

She paused dramatically, then said, "Richard."

"Richard? Are you mad?"

"I want to see him alone before he has to go back to London." Her contrite expression reminded Will of a cat after it had eaten a beloved pet bird.

"He's too old for you!" he said in an exasperated voice. "He's too . . ."

Without warning, the door swung open. "Hello," said Richard. His meaty face was flushed as he pulled off his tall hat. His pale hair lay plastered against his big skull. His blue eyes flashed. He seemed as if he were on fire. Not once did he notice Joan, trembling near the door. "Will! You've got to help me,"

Richard insisted. "You promised." Finally he glimpsed Joan.

She waved two fingers in a feeble, doe-eyed greeting. For once she seemed incapable of speaking.

Richard, still ignoring her, turned to Will. "Come into the garden, where we can talk alone."

Will untied his apron and hid it so that no one would see him in such an embarrassing outfit outside the shop. He shrugged at Joan as if to indicate that her case was hopeless. Undaunted, Joan gazed with longing out the door through which Richard had disappeared.

"Here is your opportunity," Will said in a low voice. "You can go and talk to him alone in the garden. I'll make up some excuse why I can't join him just yet."

"What will I say?" Joan replied in a flustered voice. Her face was bright red. "I can't. I simply can't."

"Will!" Richard bellowed from the garden. "I don't have all day!"

Since his sister seemed to be frozen to the shop floor, Will followed his friend through the cross-passage into the garden. A line of laundry flapped between two apple trees. Will hoped they wouldn't encounter Mother. It was a risk he knew he must take. If they stood in the street outside the shop, they might be accosted again by Biddy Price or the constable.

"What's wrong?" Will demanded. "Did the constable come to your house, too?"

"The constable?" Richard said in terror. "You said we could trust your uncle. Are we . . . are we in trouble?"

"No, no," Will said with great confidence. "Everything's fine. No one knows a thing."

"That's good. Very good." Richard wiped his forehead with his linen handkerchief. "What I came today to get from you is the sonnet you promised. Last night, remember?"

"I did?" Will felt a growing sense of dread. What other foolish things had happened during that disastrous evening?

"You said you'd compose rhymes full-fraught with serviceable vows. You said you'd write till your ink be dry and with your tears you'd moist it again. Here's some paper," said Richard. He produced a damp sheet from inside his doublet. "And here's a pen." He took a quill from his hat and uncorked the inkhorn hanging from a cord around his waist. "Now hurry! I must deliver this sonnet this very morning."

Will lowered himself onto an overturned tub. He held the paper on his knee. "On such short notice, I . . ."

"Come, Will. You wrote the best sonnets in school, remember?"

Will's shoulders sagged. He'd rather forget about those stupid verses about righteous battles, noble love, and patriotic dribble.

"You gave me your word. You said since you nearly got us both imprisoned, you owed me a favor."

"I must have been very drunk," Will grumbled. "All right, anon." He had to think. A sonnet wasn't something he could just pull out of thin air. Especially when his friend hovered about like a love-mad bee. Will dipped the tip of the quill into the open bottle of ink.

"You can do it!" Richard said impatiently.

Will stared at the blank sheet of paper. He gulped. "I'm sorry. I don't have an idea in my head."

Richard paced back and forth. "Something about absence!" he said, clapping his large hands together. "Explain why I've been gone. I still love her, but I'm not here."

"Now, that certainly doesn't sound romantic," Will said, and frowned. Even he knew that a woman would not find such a verse appealing. He tapped his forehead with the quill.

Richard's eyes gleamed with anticipation. Will tried to avoid looking at him. The idea that anyone as talented as Richard might have expected something extraordinary of him on such short notice seemed remarkable and impossible at the same time. He decided he must try. He sat up straight and recited the first thing that came into his head:

"From you I have been absent in the spring—"

"Bravo! That's a good beginning!" Richard interrupted. "Go on! Go on!"

Inspired, Will scribbled and recited at the same time:

"When proud-pied April, dressed in all his trim,
Hath put a spirit of youth in everything,
That heavy Saturn laughed and leaped with him,
Yet nor the lays of birds, nor the sweet smell
Of different flowers in odor and hue,
Could make me any summer's story tell . . ."

Will stopped, completely stumped.

"Go on! Go on!" Richard said encouragingly.

Will scratched his head. This was as far as Joan's sonnet had gone. He must think. Something more. Something more. He dipped the pen again and recited as he wrote:

"Or from their proud lap pluck them where they grew."

"Good! Good!" Richard exclaimed. "Now for the grand finish!"

Will gritted his teeth, then said with one breath,

"Nor did I wonder at the lily's white,
Nor praise the deep vermillion in the rose;
They were but sweet, but figures of delight,
Drawn after you, you pattern of all those.
Yet seemed it winter still, and, you away,
As with your shadow I with these did play."

Richard thumped him hard on the back with delight. "Wonderful!"

Will smiled. *Is it really so good?*

"I don't understand the slightest what it means," admitted Richard, "but it has a good, original, loving ring to it, don't you think? She'll adore it. Especially the part about the rose. Women love roses, don't they? We haven't much time. There's a rumor she may be going away. I have to make sure she doesn't."

"Where is she going?" Will asked after he finished the last line and carefully let the ink dry.

"Some distemperance about going to France," Richard grumbled. "You know the way women babble."

"So far away?" Will asked. France seemed as distant as the moon. He knew no one who'd ever left the shores of England. "What could possibly be in France?"

"Mere religious dotage. I plan to change her mind, of course."

"Of course." Will rolled the paper and handed it to his determined friend.

"I'm counting on your poetry to work powerful magic."

Will studied his feet. "I cannot make any guarantees," he said in a small voice.

Richard impatiently tapped the paper against his open palm. "She insists she'll go by the first of August."

"That doesn't give you much time. Only ten days," Will said, secretly glad that his employment as love poet would be so short-lived.

"I'll need five or six more installments," Richard said. "One every other day."

"Every other day?" Will felt his heart sink.

"Sending poems every day would make me look a bit desperate, don't you think?"

Will slouched forward and felt doomed.

"You'll deliver the sonnets directly to Anne Whateley in Temple Grafton," Richard said. "Her house is the only one with a slate roof and a chimney. You cannot miss it."

Will groaned. "Temple Grafton lies five miles away. I have no horse. If I walk, the way will take more than an hour."

"You'll do it for me, I know." Richard clapped Will heartily on the shoulder.

"This isn't going to work. What if she suspects something?"

"She'll never know the poem's not mine. The handwriting will be yours, of course. It'll look consistent. Will, I'm depending on you."

Will nodded reluctantly.

"As my best friend, I have your word?"

Will shook Richard's hand to seal the deal. Without bothering to say farewell, Richard took off at a run, leaped over the muck hill, and headed back to the front of the house.

When Will turned to go inside, he spied his sister's angry face staring at him from the window. She had been lurking there the entire time, hearing everything. She knew. The sonnet she had written was going to be used by the one she loved to woo another.

Chapter Nine

Will never fancied himself a go-between for Lover Not Loved and Loved Not Loving. The more he considered the idea, the more he despised it. If Richard entreated him to start arranging rendezvous and declare commendations, Will decided he'd simply refuse. He could only endure so much pain for Richard—even if he was his best friend.

A day passed. The following morning Will knew he could not put off any longer the task of writing and delivering the second love sonnet, as he had promised. After he finished the morning's work at the shop, Will walked down Henley Street toward the river to the Swan. He needed a place to compose his poem. He needed inspiration. Who was this mysterious Anne who had reduced his friend to a pathetic mass of quivering emotion? He had no idea what to write, or even how to begin.

Deep in thought, he was unaware of buzzards soaring overhead. The birds scavenged among the garbage and offal in the streets and among the ditches and gutters running before the houses, where families threw their slops. The best way to keep clear of the gutter was to walk on the inside of the sidewalk, what was known as taking the wall.

Someone coughed. Will looked up, politely doffed his cap, and allowed Mistress Fraser to pass. He ducked under one of the overhanging eaves that stuck out like a hat brim. Narrowly he missed being the direct target of a jordan, or chamber pot, dumped from above. Flies hummed. The air, hot and still, stank unbearably.

Will sensed the eyes of neighbors watching him as he walked. He made a quick bow when he spied Father's competitor Gilbert Bradley, glover.

"God speed you," Bradley said, but did not pause to chat.

Perhaps he's heard about the fight and the church warden. Will picked up his pace.

Among townsfolk, everyone knew everyone else's secrets. Everyone knew everyone else's desires. Neighbor watched neighbor for signs of sin, for breaking of rules. Will nodded to Elizabeth Pritchard, who gave him a toothless grin. She once accused

Will's mother of purposefully setting her goat upon the Pritchard's garden. Mistress Pritchard's neighbor, in turn, took her to court for allowing a scabbed, or diseased, cow on common land.

Townsfolk were regulated by one another's peering glances, by shame, and by a hundred rules enforced by the church court. There were regulations against taking in lodgers, shooting with guns or crossbows, and housing unmarried pregnant women. There were fines for not ringing pigs, failing to repair hedges, singing scandalous songs, scolding, chiding, or brawling.

Sometimes talk in town tasted as stale as pond water where flax steeped.

"He's a Lane. Lanes is like that. Ill-tempered rascals."

"That's just his way."

"She has no more sense than her mother. Cat will after kind."

Townsfolk reminded Will of horses standing side to side talking to each other, chewing cud, and observing each other's comings and goings. Yet when they looked at him, he could not help feeling naked.

Horses' hooves trampled and clip-clopped up Chapel Street. Will recognized the fine rig of Bishop Whitgift from Worcester on his way up to the vicar's house. Will slunk to the farthest edge of the narrow street. Everyone else on foot did the same. No one cheered or hailed the bishop. A few doffed their hats. Most averted their gazes.

The bishop, dressed in black, kept his sharp collar up in spite of the heat. He sat ramrod stiff and surveyed the upstairs windows of chambers. Rumor was that his glance was so ruthless, he could spot disbelievers on sight. His sense of smell was so pronounced, he could sniff out a hiding priest houses away.

Will hunkered down, hoping he would not be recognized. He had not been to church in months. No one in his family went to church anymore. Father had developed into something of an art the ability of keeping his whereabouts unknown whenever church authorities came to their house to demand payment of fines.

As the head of the household, Father was the only one who could be formally charged with disobedience. If he remained unavailable, unseen, or mysteriously absent when fine collectors came to the door, he was safe. Naturally, it didn't hurt that most of the fine collectors and government officials were Father's friends, who tipped him off when they'd be paying a visit.

Will wondered how much longer Father would be able to keep up his cat-and-mouse game with the church. For the past year visits from authorities had grown more frequent.

Finally Will reached Back Bridge Street, and he dodged safely inside the Swan. The cool air smelled of soiled rushes, old beer, and fresh meat pies. Through an open window he spied the constable strolling past. Will's heart pounded. He tried to keep himself steady. Even so, he stumbled as he crossed the room to find a table for himself. Why should he feel afraid? His sister had given the excuse he needed. He was free, wasn't he?

A group of regulars who came every day to play a clattering game of shovelboard called to one another and laughed. Nearby, another group hunched over their cards. They knew to hide their hands quickly if the church warden wandered in for a cup of claret. When Will's bench made a scraping noise, the card players looked up, recognized him, and then went back to their game.

For a moment, Will sensed a kind of peace. The Swan's darkness embraced him. Here was one place he wouldn't be judged.

"Will, you're early today," announced a cloying woman's voice.

Will's shoulders sagged. "Hello, Mopsa," he said forlornly. "I thought you were working in the evenings."

"Not today," she said, and wiped the table with a dirty rag.

Will removed a piece of paper from inside his doublet. He didn't want to have to speak to her. Not now. He studied the paper with great intensity, as if to indicate to her that he was deep in thought and busy. Very busy. He had no time for idle gossip.

She thumped a tankard of ale on the table and leaned forward, so that he could not avoid looking at her. "You seem gastful. Are you ill? Perhaps you caught a cold on the river."

Will took a sip and glanced up at her over the tankard's rim. "I look so dreadful? I am fine and fit," he said, and coughed. "You won't tell any of your customers about that little Midsummer Eve episode, I hope." Then he added in a low voice, "If certain people knew, I could be in very great trouble."

"Aye," she said. "Your secret's safe with me. All the same, you should take better care of yourself. You look tired and worn." She smiled and tousled his hair.

Will found this gesture annoying. What if she was planning on blackmailing him? Nervously he gulped his ale. In broad daylight Mopsa was not an elegant creature. Her eyes were too small. Her nose was too big. Her fingernails were dirty. She was not one to inspire a love sonnet. Perhaps he should go elsewhere to find a quiet, safer place to write. Just as he was about to rise from the bench and head for the door, Mopsa placed her hand on his arm. "Where were you three nights ago?" she asked in a low voice.

Three nights ago? Will smiled weakly. He couldn't remember. Was that the night they'd been chased through Charlecote?

"You was supposed to meet me at the stile in Badger's field."

"Oh," said Will, and took a sip from the tankard.

"You hold to your promise, don't you, Will?"

Will took another gulp and nearly choked. "Dear Mopsa!" he said and coughed. He hoped that none of the card players had heard her words. *What promise?*

Her eyes shone with happiness. "I knew you would."

Will winced. He could already feel the band of the hangman tightening around his neck. How would he ever be rid of her? "I've some work to do. Have you something for me to eat?"

"Of course," she said. Her adoring glance reminded him of the smithy, Richard Hornsby, after he had purchased a new anvil. He made everyone who passed stop to admire his new equipment. *How can anyone love something so hard, so unfeeling?* It sickened Will for a moment to think how kind Mopsa was when he treated her so badly. He was as cold as that anvil.

While she scurried to the kitchen he dipped the quill into the ink. He had to think of something to write. He scribbled: "I love you beyond expression."

What babble! He crossed it out.

"What are you describing, Will?" Mopsa placed a plate of bread and cheese on the table and inspected the page. There was no point in covering the words. She couldn't read. "Is it for me?" she asked.

He didn't answer, because his mouth was full of cheese.

"Would you like more ale?"

Will shook his head slowly. He considered Mopsa's generosity. Her great goodness of heart. Her unbounded love for him, he who was so undeserving. She would never tell Sir Lucy what he had done. How could he have been so suspicious? "Do you know you are too kind, too willing, Mopsa?"

Mopsa seemed delighted by this unusual praise. "I am your slave," she said with sincerity.

Will sighed. "Nonny, nonny."

"All right, then," she said, and gave him a confused look, "I'll tell you a trifle if that's what you want to hear. I am not your slave. I am or I am not—whatever you will. Whatever you desire." She shuffled back to the kitchen for a fresh meat pie. Her shabby pumps flip-flopped against the rush-strewn floor.

Outside, the cathedral bell rang the noon hour. Soon he would have to go back to work. Father would find out about his escape to the Swan and would patter endlessly about his shortcomings. Will glanced at the paper. He'd written almost nothing. "Your slave," he murmured, then nibbled the edge of his quill. He scratched:

> *Being your slave, what should I do but tend*
> *Upon the hours and times of your desire?*
> *I have no precious time at all to spend,*
> *Nor services to do, till you require.*

The card players stood up, stretched, and gulped down their last ale. They punched one another good-naturedly.

"Time to go back to work," said one.

"I'll wager a groat," replied his companion, "you will be late."

Will dipped the quill again and wrote:

> *Nor dare I chide the world-without-end hour*
> *Whilst I, my sovereign, watch the clock for you,*

Nor think the bitterness of absence sour
When you have bid your servant once adieu.

By the time Mopsa returned with the pie, he had finished the poem. Hastily, he tried to dry the ink by blowing on the page.

"Where are you going?" Mopsa said. "When will I see you again?"

"Soon," he replied gaily, delighted to have finally finished. He wondered how long it would take him to travel by foot to Temple Grafton and back. He pocketed the last of the bread and cheese and the meat pie, then gave Mopsa a loud smack on the cheek.

Chapter Ten

Will sprinted along Wood Street, past Rother Market, and south along Back Lane to the road west toward Shottery, and then on to Temple Grafton. The midday sun beat down unmercifully. He had to slow his steps. If only he had a horse! *An extravagance I can't afford.* His father would ask questions. He picked up his pace again.

In the middle of the road ahead, he saw what appeared to be a heap of rags. Around the heap huddled a group of shouting boys. He recognized one of the red-haired sons of John Ainge, the baker. He was a lean, crooked-toothed youth a year younger than Joan, with large feet and larger hands. "Get you gone, vagabond!" he squealed. His two pimply friends danced around and around the pile of rags. Every so often they hurled something at the pile.

"Mercy, your honor!" the pile of rags cried. "I am no witch."

"Then I condemn you for not attending church!" the baker's boy shouted, and pitched another rock. "Where is your home?"

"Gone, gone," the pile muttered pitifully. "I have no home. Leave me, sir."

"Why torment this overtrodden beggar?" Will demanded. The baker's boy was so shocked to see Will standing nearby, he didn't seem to know what to say. "Speak, fool," Will said.

"This is a dangerous vagrant," the baker's boy announced. "This beggar may have the plague or bring some mischief into town."

"Don't have no plague, sir," the pile cried.

"The plague on you, Ainge," Will said, and picked up a stone and began to toss it back and forth between his hands. He cocked his head to one side. "Do you fancy yourself a constable?"

"No," the baker's boy said nervously. His friends backed away and began running. "You cannot tell me what to do."

"Why not?"

"You are from a family of devil worshipers."

"Who says, sirrah?"

"Everyone." The boy's voice became stronger, as if he felt bolder. "You are lucky you have not been burned at the stake."

"I shall burn you at the stake if you do not shut your mouth," Will said angrily. He hurled the rock over the boy's head. The baker's son leaped like a startled hart and took off down the road. He did not look back.

The bundle of rags shook, rose, and became a bent old man with scabby sores on his bare arms. "Anything to spare to eat, your worship?" His high, thin, begging voice sounded like a child's, even though his face was deeply creased with wrinkles. His pale eyes looked blank with hunger.

Something about the beggar disturbed Will. He didn't know why. Quickly he dug inside his pocket and gave him the bread and cheese that had been a gift from Mopsa. The stranger used clawlike hands and ate so fast, Will wondered if he tasted anything.

"More?"

"That's all I have," Will said impatiently. He was wasting valuable time. He must be on his way.

"More!" The beggar shadowed him. He made a crooning sound Will had heard before. But where?

"I've no time for your mischief," Will said. "Here. Take this meat pie and begone. That's all I can give you."

The meat pie delighted the beggar, who acted as if he'd been given a handful of gold. He cradled the pie inside the folds of his rags.

"Cease following me," Will warned. He turned and began to hike toward Temple Grafton.

The beggar followed him.

"Begone!" Will shouted angrily, and ran.

The beggar laughed and called after him, "How perilous is it to choose not to love the life we're shown?"

When Will heard these words, he stopped. He turned slowly, afraid to look.

The beggar had vanished.

"The heat," Will muttered. He picked up his pace again. *Nothing more.* He tried to reassure himself. Somehow he didn't succeed.

He could not shake from his mind the words and the vision from Charlecote. *Shape-shifter.* He'd heard of such things. Nervously he broke into a lope. He was eager to have the delivery made and duty done so that he could get home before dark.

Temple Grafton was a small hamlet with only a dozen houses and one old church. Will looked about for a house with a slate roof and a chimney. Just as Richard had said, there was only one. Smoke poured from the chimney of the fairly impressive cottage. A blackbird sat on the roof watching him. Will quickly made the sign of the cross three times, took a deep breath, and knocked on the door.

He wasn't sure what a go-between did or how he should announce himself. He planned to simply make an introduction, present the verse and greetings from Richard, and rush back to town. That beggar had given him a scare. He didn't want to meet any other shape-shifters at twilight on his way home.

He knocked again. No answer. Nervously he took a peek through one of the windows. Was anyone home? And what if Anne's furious father answered? Will had never stopped to consider that Richard's suit might not be greeted with favor. He knocked once more, determined that if no one answered, he'd take his sonnet and go back to town. He'd tell Richard he tried but no one came to greet him.

Just as he was about to leave, the bolt slid inside the door. The door opened a crack. "Yes?" a woman's voice asked.

Will coughed nervously and removed his cap. "Mistress, is this the home of the Whateley family?"

"Why need you to know?"

"I am seeking to deliver something for Anne Whateley. An item of a personal nature . . . from a . . . from a friend."

The door opened wider as soon as he mentioned Anne's name. *That's better.* For the first time he could see the woman's face. The sight made him gasp. She had a pug nose and pinched, close-set eyes, like a pig's. When a sow dashed across the yard, Will started in terror. What spell had been cast upon Richard to make him fall in love with such a cursed creature?

"Anne?" Will said slowly. He reached inside his doublet to quickly deposit the paper.

The woman shook her head. Her laughter sounded musical. "I am not Anne. My sister is at prayer. I will call her for you."

Will stammered his thanks and waited nervously. He could see a farmer with a scythe across the way in the shimmering heat of a hayfield. The man mopped his brow with a rag. *He's watching me the same way folks at home watch strangers.*

"So, sir, who are you?" a dulcet voice called.

Will turned and saw a lovely woman coming closer. She seemed to float along the ground like early morning sunlight or smoke on a bright, cold day. Her hair was tucked inside a spotless, white linen coif. Around her neck hung a simple wooden cross. She carried a small prayer book in her gloved hands.

"Good afternoon, Mistress," Will said. He

removed his hat and twisted it in his hands. He could think of nothing to say. Never in his life had he seen such wondrous blue eyes. *The color of sky.* She had an aquiline nose, a full mouth, and a short upper lip that made her expression look soft and delicate.

"Good afternoon," she said, and smiled.

He watched her lips move, mesmerized. She was the fairest woman he had ever seen—as fine and free of defects as the very best tightly grained French kidskin.

She tilted her head slightly. "You have a name?"

Will blushed. His voice had vanished.

"You have come on a long journey it seems," she said patiently. "My sister says you have brought me something?" She brushed a fly from her sleeve. Her hands were impossibly small—a measure too dainty for his father's glove measuring tools.

Speak! Will cleared his throat. He wished that he had brushed himself off before he knocked on the door. "I have a sonnet for you."

"Well?" she said, waiting.

Do something! He should read the poem. He should read it someplace private. But he wasn't sure he could breathe.

"Sir, you look parched. Would you like some small beer?" Anne asked. She motioned to a bench under an ash tree. She sat down. Her sister carried a load of laundry and hung it on a nearby bush within easy earshot. Clearly, she had been instructed not to leave Anne alone with Will, a suspicious stranger.

"I am not thirsty," Will said, even though the inside of his mouth was as dry as the dusty ruts along the road. Clumsily he produced the sonnet folded within his doublet. "I have come here with a message from Richard . . . Richard Field."

When she heard this name, she smiled. "I thought Richard was gone to London."

"He is." Will straightened his back, his shoulders. *Too bad for Richard.* He smiled at her and hoped she noticed his handsome profile. "I am here to deliver his . . . his sonnet." He took a deep breath and continued. "He sends you his greetings and this poem." Without any other introduction he read the new sonnet. He recited it far too quickly—mostly out of nervousness. He did not look up except one time halfway through in order to check her lovely face. She seemed engrossed, as if she were listening to faraway music. This cheered him, even though the poem made no sense at all to him now.

"Lovely!" Anne said. "Richard is a true poet."

"He is?" Will replied, stunned.

"Such tender words." Anne reached out and took the page, folded it, and placed it inside her bodice.

Lucky paper!

"How long have you known Richard?" she asked.

Without thinking, Will frowned. He didn't like the way she said Richard's name with such softness. "All my life. We were schoolmates."

"I see," she said, and paused. "I, too, feel as if I've known him all my life. Perhaps because his poetry has caught fast my heart." She glanced down at her lap. Her eyelashes fluttered.

Will smiled with pleasure. "Who would have thought Richard could write such a masterpiece?"

She nodded, then said in a modest voice, " '*Causa latet, vis est notissima.*' "

Will felt as stunned as if she had poked him in the face with a sharp stick. " 'The cause is hidden, but the result is well known.' You read Ovid?"

Nervously she glanced over her shoulder. "I am not supposed to, although it is among my favorites. Except, of course, for the Bible."

"Of course," said Will. He couldn't believe his incredible luck. What were the chances that he would meet a beautiful, refined woman who admired the works of Ovid as much as he did?

"I am supposed to only study religious works, the *Herbal Remedies,* and that is all," she continued. "Poetry, fables, romances like Launcelot of the Lake,

Tristan and Isolde—these are forbidden. Other learning a woman needs not, Father says."

"Of course," said Will. He thought of Joan and her infatuation with love sonnets and silly ballads. She understood nothing of the depth of true literature. Not like Anne. This realization gave him an unexpected sense of delight. The idea that his writing had the power to move and transport someone as learned as Anne pleased him enormously. Perhaps his words were powerful. Perhaps they had meaning and music. Anne called them tender. She called them lovely.

Will stood and made a small bow, suddenly recalling the late hour and the fact that Father would be furious when he discovered his absence—once again.

"Where are you going?" Anne asked. Something about her voice had the sound of regret. This, too, filled him with a kind of giddy hope.

"Home," Will said.

"When will you return with more of Richard's poetry?"

"Soon." Crazy joy transported him. He felt as if he could fly back to town.

"Can you take a message?" she asked, startling him from his reverie. Her lovely face gazed up at him.

"For whom?"

She laughed. "For Richard."

"Of course." *The blackguard!* "What would you like me to tell him?"

"Ask him when I may hear more of his rare phrases."

Will felt his heart might burst with joy. "Soon. Soon, I'm sure." He lurched backward, bowing, tripping as he went. "Farewell!"

Anne waved. Her sister giggled.

Will hastened toward town as if skimming along the dirt road. He was unaware that the sky had turned gray. Fat raindrops fell. The rain sent up a sweet perfume from the dust. The drizzly meadows abounded with beauty. Why had he never noticed before such loveliness? Even the muddy, damp cows looked beautiful. Will waved at the big-eyed creatures with giddy abandon.

Anne's perfect face shone in his mind even when he closed his eyes. Will had memorized her soulful eyes, her goodness, her honesty. Surely Anne would save him. Her purity, her piety would transform him. She was everything perfect, everything good. *Everything I am not.*

He stopped midstride, suddenly aware of the truth. So this was what true love felt like!

He soared along the ground again, faster now. He

would have to find some way to have her, to woo her, to never part from her. *What wrabbed luck!* He'd fallen in love with his best friend's beloved. *Not my fault.* Richard should never have made him write the sonnet and deliver it. He should never have allowed Will to see Anne in the first place.

Chapter Eleven

Will waded through spongy, ice-cold marsh. Rain filled the soft bottom with bog water, which seeped onto the muddy road and created a river. By the time he arrived at home, he was soaked through but still happy.

He didn't hear a word Father shouted at him about irresponsibility and cursed stubbornness. He scarcely noticed the sadness in his mother's face. Even the gibes of Joan and his brothers had no effect on Will. He paid no attention to any of their under-the-breath insults.

What bib! Will ignored the nonsense talk and climbed upstairs, supperless, to the chamber he shared with his brothers. He didn't need to eat. When he removed his soggy clothing, he noticed there was an *A* and half of a *W* providentially made upon his breeches, plain to view in any man's sight. The letters were made of mire and seemed a kind of miracle. *A,* he decided, was for Anne. The *W* was for Whateley.

This discovery filled him with joy. He looked upon it to be a sign of Providence. *It foretells something in my apprehension.* He laid his clothing carefully out to examine. "The smallest of God's Providences should not be passed by without observation," he proclaimed. Such wisdom surprised him. Already Anne's goodness was having an effect, he decided. *I must see her tomorrow.*

That night after everyone was fast asleep, he wrote a dozen sonnets by the light of a burning rush set in tallow. It was a dangerous undertaking. Such lights had been known to spark fires in thatched roofs and destroy entire town blocks. Will believed the risk was worth it. His affections ran out violently after Anne, and he had to express himself. How could he be content until he saw her again?

While his brothers slept, he scribbled. Soon he lost track of time, entranced as he was by language— the magic and music of words that sometimes made no sense. Page after page he scribbled, using grand phrases that rolled wildly from his tongue—"blazon of sweet beauty's best" and "prophetic soul."

The way Anne had reacted to his sonnet amazed and frightened him. It was as if he'd discovered that

he had some strange power he didn't know about—
like bending metal with his bare hands or moving
rocks with his vision. Again and again he considered
how her face had looked when he read to her. The
odd and faraway expression that made her seem so
startled, so overwhelmed.

While this newfound power gave him a certain
pride, it also made him nervous. What if he couldn't
repeat the magic? What if the magic only came once?
What if Anne loved the first poem best—the one that
was mostly Joan's, not his?

He lost his nerve and suddenly felt unable to
write anything. *Perhaps I'm a fraud.*

A mouse skittered across the floor and startled
him. Through a chink in the wall made of brittle wattle and daub, Will gazed desperately at the moon. Isn't
that what lovers did when they needed inspiration?

He put his pen to paper again, but nothing came.
What does she think of me? He sighed and felt very
sorely troubled. He would not be content until he
saw her again.

Will tapped his pen against the table edge. Rest-
lessly, he stood up and tried to remember what the
little man had told him about the way to stand, to
move. He assumed the regal stance of Sir Lucy.
"Calling my officers about me in my branched velvet

gown," he said half-aloud, "having come from the daybed where I slept. I frown, perchance wind up my watch, play with some rich jewel. Then I—"

"Still awake?" Joan hissed.

Will jumped and awkwardly tried to turn over the pages facedown on the table.

"The moon must be making you mad. Do you know you were talking to yourself in a strange manner?" She stood in the entrance to the chamber with a lit taper in her hand.

"Be gone, wanton," he replied angrily.

She stepped closer. "What are you writing? Something secret, perhaps. It's very long, isn't it?"

Will hurriedly rolled up the papers.

"Some sonnets, I'd wager," she said, her eyes narrowing. "Let me have a look. Perhaps I can help you make them better."

"Why should you do that?"

"My verse is better than yours."

"Perhaps," Will said. He smiled and refused to unroll the paper. "You're a great boaster for an ignorant girl."

Joan glowered at him. "If I were a man, I could write anything I wanted. I could go to the university. I could publish books. I could leave this town and be somebody."

Will leaned back and stared at her in frank amazement.

"Stop looking at me as if I were mummying."

Will gave an unconvincing laugh. He wanted to make fun of Joan, but her talk of writing and universities and publishing books and leaving town had made him speechless. Even though Will had been considered a most promising scholar, he was forced to end his schooling when he was fourteen. Bitterly he recalled the day his father told him there was no money to send him to the university. The loss of Mother's land, his father's fall from power as bailiff, his loss of status as a man of substance—all these catastrophic events Father called the Great Misfortune. The Great Misfortune, Will decided, had swept away his birthright, his inheritance, his future. For Joan there would be such a small dowry, who would marry her? "Life isn't fair, you know," Will grumbled.

"Aye," Joan agreed. "I heard how Richard woos another."

"So it would seem," replied Will. With some exasperation he ran his fingers through his hair.

Joan sniffed. "He only has ten days, isn't that what he said?" Joan replied hopefully. "He may fail."

Ten days! Will tapped his quill on the bottle and corked it. He hoped his horror didn't show. What if *he* failed? He had to dash off some more poems and tell Anne himself that he loved her. He'd convince her not to go to France. Tomorrow. He'd go tomorrow and tell her. "Good night!" Will said cheerfully, hoping his sister would take his meaning and leave him in peace.

Instead, Joan drew with her toe the shape of a heart in the dust on the floor. "Please tell me when Richard is to return."

"You should give up these hooked affections," Will said in a gruff voice. "He loves another. She is a great beauty."

Joan pouted. "What is beauty but a bait to entice?"

Will refused to think of his beloved Anne as something as lowly as bait. "I will let you know as soon as Richard says he's coming," Will replied hurriedly. "Now will you leave so that I may think in quiet?"

Joan refused to budge. "Do you ever wonder," she said slowly, "why we were put on this earth?"

Will felt his skin crawl. "No, of course not. What a stupid idea. Will you go? I'd like to—"

"If I had a different name," Joan interrupted, "I wonder if I might have more luck with love. Joan is such a plain, plodding name."

"It fits you."

"I should like it better to be called Rosalind."

"Rosalind!" Will whistled softly. He arched one critical eyebrow. "By my fay, a goodly name!"

Joan scowled. "Fie on you!" she said in a hurt voice. "You are mad *and* cruel." She turned and trudged from the chamber.

For a moment, Will felt sorry that he'd been so heavy-handed with her. And yet he believed it was his duty as her older brother to make her understand the ways of the world. *Better that she knows her place and keeps it.* She was plain Joan—not exotic Rosalind. Their father was deep in debt and in terrible trouble with the authorities. With such a pitiful dowry as their family could afford, what husband could be found for Joan who would not be scared off by her learning? No one was impressed by a homely wench who was stark mad or wonderful forward. A girl who could read and write poetry was useless unless she happened to be a queen, a gentlewoman, or a lady. *Or someone as beautiful and cultured and well-off as Anne,* Will thought dreamily.

He glanced at the rolled-up paper and suddenly felt very weary. He blew out the burning rush, intending to nap, then wake up and write some more. *Winking will do me good.* He laid his forehead on the crook of his arm. In a moment, he was fast asleep.

* * *

During the next two days Will delivered six poems to Anne's home in Temple Grafton. They seldom spoke more than a few words, yet each time he came, he felt consumed by the need to see her lovely face as soon as she said farewell and shut the door. He knew he was in love because he scarcely noticed the miles he trudged back and forth.

That evening, after walking nearly twenty miles and putting in two full days of work, Will was exhausted. He tried to stay awake to finish more sonnets, but he could not keep his eyes open. He fell asleep with his pen in his hand.

Plunk. Plunk-a-plunk. Plunk.

Will sat up, alert. What time was it? He rubbed his eyes with his inky fist.

Plunk. Plunk-a-plunk. Plunk.

Will opened the shutter. On the ground below, he spied a squat shape waving furiously from the shadows.

"Come on, man!"

It was Uncle Hal. Will could tell by the way his uncle wobbled as he bent to pick up another rock from the street that he was drunk, as usual.

Soon he'd wake the whole house, then the whole neighborhood. His uncle was already in trouble for slandering the game wardens' wives. Disrupting the peace after last curfew bell would land him in the stocks. Will couldn't argue with him from this distance, so he slithered out the window and shinnied down a tree to the street.

"What are you doing?" Will murmured. He glanced over his shoulder up the dark street. "Go home. You're going to get in trouble."

"Not me," Uncle Hal said, and hiccuped. "I am on a commission from God."

Will rolled his eyes. He had accompanied his uncle on other missionary expeditions before. They always ended up in some unholy, unexpected destination. "Follow me," Hal hissed. He grabbed Will by the arm and dragged him down Henley Street to the Guild Pits behind the Angel. The inn had few people staying there these days. Travelers were warned by townsfolk that the inn's owner had been excommunicated for not going to church. "Here! Over here!" Hal insisted.

He crawled behind William Smith's shed and pointed. Will gasped. A dead body leaned on one elbow, propped against the mud wall. "Who—who is it?" Will stammered.

"Whitgift!" Uncle Hal said triumphantly.

Horrified, Will took a step closer. He didn't believe his uncle would actually kill the bishop, even if he did hate him with a burning passion. Will gave the bishop a poke. His head rolled and fell off. "It's not real!" Will whispered with relief.

"Of course not," Uncle Hal crowed.

Will clamped his hand over his uncle's mouth. "Quiet! Now what are you doing? What mischief are you about this time?"

"A simple, harmful prank." Uncle Hal rubbed his hands together with eagerness. "Tomorrow is Thursday—market day. A perfect moment for my stratum. We take Whitgift and we dress him in this." Uncle Hal produced from inside his bulky doublet a dress that had belonged to his late wife. "Then we lock him in the stocks, which for once are empty. What do you say? Serves him right, the blackguard."

Will couldn't help himself. He liked the idea. Whitgift had made so many lives miserable since he'd been appointed by the Queen. His arrogance and pride had destroyed recusant and churchgoer alike. "We don't have much time," Uncle Hal said in a low voice. "Will you help me?"

"I suppose," Will replied, unwilling to allow his uncle to botch the plan and end up in jail. "But we have to hurry."

Will and Uncle Hal quickly dressed the dummy, which had been made from old barley sacks stuffed with straw. Somehow, Uncle Hal, always a bit of a thief, managed to find a bishop's hat—just lying about. This was the crowning touch. Quietly they crept along Windsor Street, the back way to Rother Market Cross and the empty stocks.

"Grab her ankles, will you?" Uncle Hal said. "She's a frisky wench!" They shoved the awkward dummy into place and plunked the bishop's hat on its head with little ceremony. "And just in case nobody knows *who* is so preciously bedecked, I made this." Uncle Hal took a sign from his doublet and strung it round the dummy's neck.

OUR GODSHIP, WHITGIFT

Will stood back and examined the masterpiece. The dummy was far more daring and creative than the time he and his uncle dismantled the bailiff's cart and hung it at the top of a tree, or the time they filled the constable's well with eels. Of course, if they were caught, they'd face terrible punishment. Somehow the threat of danger made their prank all the more exhilarating.

"I hear something," Will whispered. He yanked his uncle by the elbow.

"What?" Hal demanded. "It's a good job, isn't—"

"Hush!" Will clamped his hand over his uncle's mouth. Footsteps thudded closer and closer. In the darkness it was impossible to see which direction someone was coming. "Not another word!" Will hissed in his uncle's ear. "Follow me." Desperately, he yanked and pulled his uncle into the shadows.

"Who goes there?" a voice called. A feeble torch moved up and down. "State your business." A cat yowled. Something splashed. A terrible odor began to fill up the night air. "Your last chance," the night watchman shouted in a muffled voice. "What is that awful stink?" he muttered with a kerchief held tight to his nose and mouth. Turning, he scurried away.

It took all of Will's self-control to keep from making gagging noises. In their hurry to escape, he and his uncle had accidentally knocked over a barrel of offal.

"It's a good thing I'm well-used by drink. I can scarcely smell that ripe, puking odor!" Hal declared, staggering away with Will as fast as he could.

"Go home now before someone spies you here," Will begged.

Hal chuckled. "If we're lucky, we won't end up in jail."

Will couldn't think of a jovial response. Something weighed heavily on his heart. Then he remembered. Anne. He was back to his old, evil ways. His life of crime and sin. "Uncle, I must go," Will whispered. "We'll part here."

"Take care!" Uncle Hal called in a low voice. "All sins and quarrels are reckoned in church court books. Spidery handwriting they have. Spidery handwriting because they are spiders!" He guffawed at his cleverness.

Will gently guided his uncle in the direction he needed to head home—up Rother Street back to the Guild Pits and then on the road to Snitterfield that led north behind the Angel. "Get you gone, Uncle."

"You, too, boy. Before it's too late." Uncle Hal waved a faltering farewell and stumbled on his way.

Something made Will shiver when he heard these words.

Chapter Twelve

Will awoke before dawn the next morning to help Father cart their wares to the High Cross House at Rother Market. On his way to market, Will could not avoid hearing their neighbor Wedgewood, the tailor, who stood outside the blacksmith's. Wedgewood talked sedition and treason with shears and measures in one hand.

"Who dares defame Whitgift?" said Richard Hornsby, the blacksmith, who listened openmouthed.

"In a dress," added Wedgewood solemnly. As usual, he was wearing his slippers on the wrong feet. "Somebody put the bishop in the stocks dressed as a *woman*! I saw it for myself on High Street."

Hornsby shook his head. "The world is going in a bad way when people have no respect for religious authorities."

Will hurried past and tried hard to make sure they could not see his grinning expression. *The trick worked!* He rushed to Rother Market to set up their display of gloves, belts, purses, on wooden shelves near the High Cross.

The town boomed with the shrieks of animals and the loud voices of farmers, merchants, and shoppers. Countryfolk wandered into town wide-eyed, smelling of sweat and cattle.

Like the other glovers, Will and Father hovered behind the glove display at High Cross. Nearby were sellers of hide and lowing, penned cattle. Flies swarmed. The morning air reeked of manure. "Stand clear! Stand clear!" hollered the drivers who unloaded salt wains, carts filled with salt.

The chaos of animals and people, goods and food, was repeated on each of the major thoroughfares. Pigs squealed on Ely Street. Sheep gamboled stupidly in temporary pens set up on Sheep Street. Horses nervously pawed the ground on Church Way. Farmers with wagons heavily laden with grain, commonly called corn, stood idly on Corn Street. Here, salters and sugarers hawked their wares. Ironmongers and nailers, collar makers and ropers lined Bridge Street. The men and women who hawked white meat—butter, cheese, eggs—and those who sold wick yarn for candles set up shop at the Chapel or White Cross. Tanners occupied the guildhall, where sealers marked the leather.

Children raced through the crowd, chased by barking dogs. Roaming peddlers howled songs. From their packs they displayed coifs of black and tawny; handkerchiefs; garters; gloves; laces; white inkle, or tape; thread; buttons; pins; and thimbles. The blind harper found a safe place near High Cross to strum and sing an old ballad. On the next street John Taborer played a lilting song on a drum and pipe.

The whole world seemed to have come to market today. The place thrummed and hummed with talk and gossip about only one thing: the scandal of Bishop Whitgift. Will tried to appear unconcerned and ordinary. He must not give himself away. Spies lurked everywhere.

"Makers of slanderous libel!" Widow Bromley said as she bustled up to their glove display. "Did you hear?"

Will nodded and kept his gaze away from the prattling woman. "They say the archbishop is fit to murder the terrorist who left such an ugly symbol. We may have a hanging yet. And how is your mother today, boy?"

"Fine, madame," Will said. He pulled at the collar of his shirt with the tip of one finger. He could feel

Widow Bromley's eyes peering about his clothing for some popery—a crucifix, perhaps.

"Haven't seen you in church this past Sabbath." She picked up a pair of fine gloves and held them to her nose.

"I've been sick," said Will, and coughed to prove he was telling the truth. Then he thought of Anne and his vow to lead a more upright, honest life. "I intend on going this Sunday and every Sunday thereafter."

Father, who shuffled some sheepskin gloves, shot Will a surprised glance. Will ignored him.

"These gloves have the scent of Spanish perfume," said the widow, who picked up a pair that smelled as sweet as damask roses.

"The Spanish do make the finest perfume," replied Father in his most helpful voice. As soon as he spoke, he turned pale. He seemed to immediately realize his mistake.

"The Spanish make the finest perfume?" said the widow. "I always thought the English to be superior in their perfuming skills."

"They are. They are indeed," said Father hurriedly. "What I meant was—"

"Do you favor the Spanish, sir?" Widow Bromley asked abruptly. "They are Catholic. They are the enemy. I hope you are not a traitor, sir."

"I am not," said Father. He spoke in a low voice as if to calm Widow Bromley so that she might not bark louder and draw a crowd. "What I meant was—"

"The Spanish," she interrupted, "are dirty foreigners who wish to take over the throne. Who wish to wreak havoc on us—leaving behind sordid symbols to shake our faith. They are terrorists, sir."

Will watched Father squirm. He prayed to himself that Widow Bromley would go away. "Could it be a local prank? Not planted by the Spanish at all," said Will, smiling in his most charming manner.

The widow snorted. She'd have none of his smooth smirkiness. "Such an awful symbol is too ridiculous for one of our own to have made." Her voice became increasingly shrill, her gestures more dramatic. "We may be at war soon. And I think it only right. Those papist transgressors will learn their lesson then. A young man like you should sign up. Join the Queen's army. Defend your country. Go to Spain and kill some heathens."

Will coughed pathetically. "I have five more years of my apprenticeship to fulfill, madame."

The widow looked at Will, then turned to Father and said in a haughty manner, "It's a disgrace to our town, to our country, to our religion. Did you see that dress?"

"I've never seen the bishop look so fashionable," Father replied, and chuckled.

Widow Bromley looked at him in horror. "You should be more patriotic. God save England! God save the Queen!" She turned on the downtrodden heels of her best shoes and marched away.

"Why'd you bait her like that, Father? We'll never hear the last of it," Will said. He tried to avoid his father's direct gaze, certain he would see through him and sense the truth.

Father sighed. "Will, you are starting over as of today."

"Starting over?" Will said nervously. *What's he babbling about now?*

"Today you begin a new regimen," Father continued. His expression became sterner as he spoke. "No slinking off to the taverns. No skulking about, avoiding work. No coming in late in the morning and leaving early. You will do an honest day's work so that you will learn the true meaning of life."

"Yes, Father," Will droned. "Yes, Father."

"You need to grow up now, Will," Father said darkly. "Everyone in town is talking about your behavior. You're an embarrassment to me, to the family."

Will knew better than to protest. It was only because he was the eldest that Father assumed the business would be his one day. Running the shop should one day be the work of his other brothers. Certainly Gilbert could do a better job than Will. How would Will ever be able to tell Father he didn't want to be a glover?

"Are you listening to me?" Father demanded. "You've disappeared countless times over the past two days. I didn't know where you went or when you were coming back. You can barely keep your eyes open when you sit down. I want you to stop gadding about after one giglot and another. Keep your mind on the business."

Will gave Father a hurt look. *Giglot indeed!* Anne was no disreputable wench.

"I have a delivery for you to make as soon as the market bell rings at eleven," Father continued. "An important delivery. And I want none of your malingering or dalliance today, do you understand?"

Will sighed. When would Father begin to treat him like a grown man?

"I have mourning gloves for you to deliver to the Hathaway home in Shottery. They are a respectable family. Master Hathaway just passed away, God rest his soul."

Will barely listened. He was trying to consider how far Shottery was from Temple Grafton. Inside his doublet were three more sonnets ready for delivery. He could take the footpath to Shottery and when he was finished, walk west to Temple Grafton.

Somehow he felt certain that if he didn't see Anne soon, he'd die. *Seven days.* Seven days was all he had left to convince her of his love.

"I'll go, sir," Will said reluctantly. "But I don't see why Joan can't make the delivery."

"You are the representative of the shop. You are my eldest son. You must go in my stead and try for once to be civil. This is a family of consequence who may become important customers."

Will stepped out from behind the glove display and scowled. Since when did impressing families of consequence concern Father? Lately, Father only did what he pleased.

It was Father who had announced five years ago, when Whitgift became bishop, that this was the beginning of the Great Misfortune. Their lives would never be the same again. They'd stopped going to church. Father, once politically powerful in his furred gown and special ring, refused to attend meetings of the aldermen and became an outcast. He wouldn't pay taxes and began evading the law. Little by little, their business failed. Wool brogging, illegal and now under investigation by the Queen's spies, had been completely shut down. The family's once bright future looked bleak.

It had been Father's stubbornness that had caused them to lose nearly all their wealth, land and reputation. *Just because of principle,* Will thought angrily. *What would be so difficult to pretend to be a good Protestant and follow the Queen's commandments?*

Will jammed the package under his arm and pushed his way through the crowds at Rother Market. He headed south on Rother Street to the footpath. From the hedges birds sang. It was a mile to the Hathaway family home through open fields. He tried to think of something pleasant as he walked. Something besides Father and his conscience.

Heat shimmered above the yellowing stalks of rye, which made brittle songs in the wind. It would be harvesttime soon, even though the air still smelled sweet with the fragrance of summer. Will sighed, thinking of Anne. He should go and see her this very afternoon—in spite of what Father had said about "starting over."

From a distance the twelve-room Hathaway house with its thatched roof looked as broad and rounded as a great loaf of bread. The place was one of the biggest homes in Shottery, though Will had never been inside. It seemed like a grand house, much grander than Anne Whateley's home.

Hathaway had been a well-to-do yeoman farmer who refused to have much to do with the people in town. He'd married twice, and eight of his children lived here with his second wife, newly widowed. Will knocked on the massive door. He waited and brushed a fly from his face. Morning glories the color of deep water climbed a trellis. He hummed and waited, wondering if he might be interrupting the wake.

Death was a frequent visitor in town. The wake would be held in the Hathaway home, followed by a funeral procession to the churchyard. No doubt it would be a simple, stark burial. The Hathaways were staunch Protestants. Will sniffed. In this heat they wouldn't be able to keep the body unburied long. Will knocked again. Was no one home? Finally the great wooden door opened.

"Hello?" someone greeted him from the cool darkness. A woman appeared in the doorway. She had a plain face with high cheekbones. *No beauty.* Will couldn't help but compare her with Anne Whateley. A linen coif covered the woman's head, and she wore an apron of fine linen. From her belt hung ribbons attached to a fancy feather fan, a pomade ball made of perfumed herbs, and a mirror. She inspected Will closely, in a way that made him feel uncomfortable. "You are?" she demanded.

Self-consciously, Will turned the package over and over in his hands. "The glover's son. I come with a delivery from Henley Street in town. Sorry for your loss. My family's condolences." *How stupid I sound!* He ordinarily did not appear this shy, this idiotic. It was her unflinching gaze that disquieted him. He glanced quickly at her face again and noticed that she had soft, full lips.

"Come inside," she said in a matter-of-fact tone. "Perhaps you do not remember me. I am Anne. I once pulled you from the top of a stile when you were too fearful to cross in a long dress."

Will felt his face flush hot. He didn't want to think of himself in the embarrassing childish outfit— the long clothes both boys and girls had to wear until they reached the age of seven. He pursed his lips. What did he care what she thought? *She's old. Very old.*

He stepped inside the cross-passage and into the high-ceilinged hall to the left. It was cool and dark and smelled heavily of flowers and smoke and something else sweet and rotten—death. As his eyes grew accustomed to the dimness he could see the shape of a body resting on a long table draped with a plain linen cloth. Another cloth covered the dead man's face. Nearby, several women sat weeping quietly.

Anne gestured toward the body. "My father. May he rest in peace," she said without a tinge of sadness in her voice. "The burial is today."

Will made a little bow to pay his respects. He almost unconsciously made the sign of the cross, then he thought better of it when he remembered that the Hathaways despised Catholicism. He stood beside the body for a moment. His lips moved as if murmuring a prayer.

When he finished, he glanced at Anne again. While he was supposed to be praying, he secretly calculated her age. She must have been six or eight years older than he was. He didn't know her from school, or from church or town. She seldom came to Henley Street. He'd seen her a few times on market day. She was older than Richard, older than most of his close friends. A mysterious, unnoticed presence up until this moment. When he inhaled, he sensed her fragrance. Violets.

Anne kept staring at him. To hide his shyness, he inspected her bare hands. They were nervous, fluttering hands, ringless and milk white. Not a trace of the roughness of the wife or daughter of a farmer.

Clearly, she was unaccustomed to hard work. "What kind of gloves do you make?" she demanded.

"Gloves so delicate and thin they can fit folded inside a walnut shell."

She scowled. "You lie."

Will shrugged sheepishly. "But I can tell a great deal from a person's gloves."

Anne stared at her dead father. "What could you tell about me?"

"Your characteristics, who you are, what you'd like to be. It's all in how you carry your gloves, how you wear them," Will said. He couldn't help himself. He kept talking in front of dead Master Hathaway. Although he spoke complete nonsense, he couldn't stop. The silence was too awful. "I can tell who you are by the manner in which you put your gloves on or take them off. The way you let them rest beside you, where they lie like casts of your own hands."

Her frank laughter startled him. She studied him carefully. "Perhaps," she murmured. "Come this way." She motioned across the hall to the cross-passage, where pans clanged and banged. The smoky kitchen most likely. Harsh voices rang out—the angry words of a loud woman. A child with tangled hair darted through the doorway and dodged past Will. Another child wailed. "My stepbrother and stepsister," Anne said with a kind of weariness.

From inside the kitchen emerged the sound of more crashing and the smell of roasting meat. A woman shrieked, "Fie on you and your laziness!"

Anne took the package of gloves from Will. As she did, she brushed her hand against his. Something like a shock shot up his arm and into his shoulder. For a second too long, she rested her hand on his sleeve. "You have grown up to be a handsome man," she said quietly. "It is a good thing I helped you down off that stile."

Will felt as if something burned around his neck, closing around his throat and choking him. He could think of no reply. *"It is a good thing I helped you down . . ."* Nervously he wiped sweat from his forehead. He did it quickly so she wouldn't notice.

"Anne! Anne, where are you?" the woman cried from the kitchen.

Anne acted as if she didn't hear. Slowly she unwrapped the paper and inspected the fingers of the mourning gloves. They were embroidered at the wrist with small, delicate flowers. She held the gloves to her face as if to smell them. A smile came to her lips, and her face seemed less severe. For a moment, Will tried to see the hair tucked inside her cap. It was dark hair, perhaps. Her lashes were full and dark. Her eyes were the color of ice.

"Sorry for your troubles," he murmured again, and stumbled toward the door. He struggled with the latch.

She moved closer to him and slowly slid the bolt. As she did, he smelled violets again. Early spring violets. The scent made him dizzy. He couldn't be sure, but in that instant of her unlatching the door in the darkness of the cross-passage, she stepped forward and placed her fluttering left hand with some alarming certainty for a moment—was it that long?—inside his doublet and pressed dangerously against the small of his back.

She looked as if she was amused by his astonished glance. "I will see you again," she said.

The door swung open, and he fled.

Chapter Thirteen

He tore along the Shottery footpath toward town. Without stopping, he ran past bay trees and farms that reeked of silage, past dusty briars and a lone magpie sitting on a fence post. *"You've grown up to be a handsome man."* Had she really said that? He couldn't be sure. She'd touched him. He thought that was true as well, but then again his imagination was powerful.

He streaked past a pitchfork stuck in the ground. Past an ash tree flailing in the wind. The tree's limbs reminded him of the crooked arms of an old woman. He scorched along the ground with even greater speed. He felt as if he were burning. Flames seemed to lick his cheeks; singe his arms, his legs; and crisp his hair.

From the corner of his eye, Will spotted someone watching him from a nearby field. The stooped figure carried a staff and seemed to be observing Will carefully. Will did not recognize him. The man neither lifted his hand nor signaled a greeting. He simply stared. Overhead, a buzzard soared in the wind, wings steady as a kite.

Will slowed to a lope and kept his eye on the man. *Just a shepherd.* All the same, he didn't like the way the man kept studying him, as if he were a game warden. *I've done nothing wrong.*

When Will couldn't see the fellow anymore, he felt free and weightless. He thought of Ovid. There was a shepherd in his poem, wasn't there? A shepherd who watched and was amazed. Will stretched his arms like a buzzard. He might be Icarus, the mortal who tried to fly using wings his father had fashioned from feathers, wax, and twine. Of course, he would be cleverer than Icarus. He'd avoid soaring too close to the sun or plunging too close to the ocean.

As he strode along he chanted from *Metamorphoses:*

> *"Some shepherd rests his weight upon his crook,*
> *Some ploughman on the handles of his plowshares,*
> *And all look up, in absolute amazement,*
> > *at those airborne above.*
> *They must be gods!"*

To be a god! Will felt something tingle even now at the base of his spine where her hand had touched him. Some dangerous game of flying too close to the sun.

Then he remembered. The sonnets! Instinctively, his hand slipped inside his doublet to make sure the pages were still safe. He was almost home, and he'd forgotten to deliver Anne's new sonnets. It was too late to go to Temple Grafton. Father was expecting him back in the shop. He trotted along, determined to make the delivery first thing tomorrow morning.

Late that afternoon in the shop, Will was about to close the shutters for the day when he saw an old man sidle up to the window and peer inside. One of his eyes was milky-colored and useless, so he tilted his head sideways. In profile his face appeared so dark and furrowed, he looked as if he'd been tanned with oak bark.

At first Will thought the ragged, hobbling man must be a beggar. He was about to hurry him away from the shop door when the old man spoke. "You are Will?" he asked.

Will started. How did he know his name? Will had never seen the man before. "Tell me what you want," Will demanded nervously.

"I have something for you."

Another shape-shifter? "Come inside." Will glanced up and down bustling Henley Street. He didn't like the idea of witnesses. Urgently he motioned for the man to enter the shop doorway.

The man shook his head. He took Will's arm in his bony, dirty hand and pressed a small piece of paper, folded and sealed with a red wax seal, into Will's palm. Then the man quickly disappeared into the crowd.

Everything had happened so quickly, Will couldn't be sure anyone else saw what happened. He closed his fingers around the paper and stepped inside the empty shop. He shut the door. He latched the shutters. With shaking hands, he examined the seal. The flourishing letter *A*. He used his thumb to break the red wax and opened the paper.

In penmanship of extravagant loops and backward rushing curls, the message read simply:

Meet me in the field near Two Elms at midnight.
—A

Will's heart thumped wildly. Two Elms was outside town, near the road to Temple Grafton. This must have been written by Anne, the greatest love of his life. He'd never seen her handwriting before, but he was sure it must be from her. His mind raced. How amazing that she'd seen through his ruse and penetrated the truth! Obviously, she'd sensed that the sonnets were not written by Richard. They were written by Will, inspired by the passion he felt for her.

Dramatically, Will placed his hand over his chest. Across the room he could see his reflection in the mirror. He stepped closer to the glass and repeated the gesture. Yes, he certainly did look lovesick. Anyone could see that. Maybe it was his smoldering eyes that had given him away.

He smiled. There was something delightfully bold about Anne's suggested plan. *"Meet me in the field near Two Elms at midnight."* Who would have predicted that someone so obedient and demure would ever suggest something so forbidden? A proper young lady never traveled alone at night after the curfew bell. Obviously she was acting out of desperation. How remarkable that she was willing to expose herself to such danger! There could be no better proof, Will thought, that she loved him. The peril of their rendezvous made it seem that much more thrilling.

Will picked up the broom and began sweeping out the day's dirt. Suddenly he stopped. What if she'd sent the message to speak to him about Richard? What if this meeting had nothing to do with Will but had everything to do with his oafish friend? The idea was too awful. He'd have to play the part of the helpful listener. He'd have to offer a steady shoulder so that she could cry and weep and wail. Of course, that would not be so terrible.

And yet, and yet . . . His thoughts were tortured with every kind of story, every kind of disappointing possibility. He imagined she didn't come to Two Elms that night. She was kidnapped by thieves on the road from Temple Grafton. She was attacked by wild dogs. She was betrayed by her sister, who locked her in her room and starved her to death. And on and on and on.

By the time Joan shouted inside the shop that supper was ready, Will was racked with doubt and melancholy.

"What ails you?" Joan demanded as he shut the shop door.

"Nothing," Will said in a gloomy voice. "I'm fine."

Daylight faded far too slowly as the family gathered to eat their evening meal of bread and pottage, a kind of porridge with a few vegetables and a scant amount of pork stewed together.

"Where's Will?" Mother demanded. "Our food will soon be cold. Will!"

"Yes, madame," Will said, and shuffled into the room.

" 'He comes, he comes, our hero, hero comes,' " announced Father from a favorite Mummer's Play scene as Will took his seat on the bench. " 'Sound, oh, sound the trumpet, and beat—' Now your turn, Gil."

" 'Oh, beat the drum,' " Gilbert said with delight

while Richard rapped the table hard with his spoon. " 'Loud along the shore the cannons roar, Walk in the King—' "

" 'Along the pretty hair!' " interrupted Richard.

" 'Pretty shore,' " Gilbert corrected.

Richard pouted. "That's what I said."

"Now, gentlemen and dear ladies, may we enjoy our evening grace?" Father said, and bowed his head.

Will ate, but he tasted nothing. He felt immune to everything but the passage of time. He could hardly bear to wait for midnight. Everything in his life seemed to hang in the balance of the clock, the hour, the cathedral bell.

Until midnight he barely breathed. He felt as if he was not alive at all, but only one waiting to be reborn. He pretended to sleep on his pallet, still dressed in his clothing. Finally, when he heard his brothers snoring soundly, he crept from his bed and expertly lowered himself down the elm outside the window. His escape was flawless. No one saw him as he dashed down Rother Street, along Green Hill Street, and then through the pitch-dark Back Lane.

Beyond the lane were fields of hay and barley. He hurried along until he reached Two Elms near the road to Temple Grafton. He peered hard through the darkness for the shape of someone waiting.

No one.

He hopped over a fence near Two Elms and began to move with great caution into the field. Crickets chirped. The tall grass, wet with dew, soaked his legs. He scanned every direction but could see no one. He waited, listening to his breath coming in and out. *She isn't coming.*

When he felt he could not stand the humiliation and disappointment any longer, he turned to leave the field and walk back toward the road. Despair overwhelmed him. Even the merry movement of fireflies darting past seemed to ridicule his sorrow.

And then, just as he trudged past what looked like a hedge, he heard something.

"Will?" someone hissed. "Is that you?"

Suddenly Will felt frightened. He didn't recognize the voice. Was this some kind of trick?

"Over here," the woman's voice insisted. Her laughter sounded like water, like the river when it brooded and snapped around log snags and rocks. That was when he knew for sure. It was Anne Hathaway, not Anne Whateley, who waited for him among the shadows.

At this point, he could have turned away. He could have made some brief, quiet, polite excuse and departed. If he'd been a true gentleman, he might have apologized, then insisted that he escort her home again to Shottery, say farewell, and be done with it.

But he didn't. Instead, moving as if in a dream, he entered the shadows with wings of wax, twine, and feathers.

Frogs croaked. He followed the voice until he nearly stumbled upon her beneath a tree. She'd spread a blanket there. He felt its rough edge, a rumpled mass where his feet stopped. He couldn't breathe. He knew she was seated nearby because he smelled violets.

"Well?" she asked. Just like that. Not a question but a command really. Her voice wasn't a whisper. Without wanting to, he glanced over his shoulder into the darkness. What if someone had followed him? What if someone heard her? She was, after all, a respectable woman from a family of consequence.

Will didn't know what to do.

"Sit down," she commanded.

He removed his hat and ducked down on the blanket. Immediately he felt her hand on his leg.

They didn't speak after that. He forgot all fear, and in his eagerness he found himself fumbling with everything. His laces, his breeches. He was glad it was too dark to see if she might be smiling, amused by his clumsiness. More than anything, he wished to appear practiced in lovemaking. After all, he'd had plenty of opportunities with Mopsa and the others, lifting their skirts behind the tavern, beside the haycock, or against cellar doors. It was always quick, pleasurable—a kind of release that never lasted longer than a barmaid's break from the tavern or a wench's noontime rest from fieldwork.

Will kissed her hard on the mouth and was surprised when she took both sides of his face in her violet-scented hands as if to slow him, to somehow dodge the bruising kisses. In spite of the urgency, he discovered he must slow all his caresses even though he was certain he might explode like parcels of fireworks. And yet what surprised him was that her maddening caresses seemed to make more pleasurable that which was ordinarily simply a release. A brief abandonment.

In a wild, final moment he saw nothing, felt nothing except a blaze of energy, like disappearing over the edge of a cliff. Like flying.

Amazed, befuddled, he finally caught his breath and discovered he was still earthbound. Tall, whispering grass bent in the breeze. He rolled over, feeling the prickly blanket against his face. He was aware she was still there breathing, smelling damp. Her breath moved like little wind on his arm.

A branch broke. He lifted his head to peer into the darkness. If they were caught, there'd be a terrible price to pay.

"Who's that?" he whispered.

"No one," she hissed, and drew him toward her. And again, with some surprising energy, she invited him to repeat the performance he'd just given. Happily he complied. He was amazed and delighted that this time he could actually plunge into some new, unknown depth and return whole. Time vanished. He forgot to worry about the noise of possible intruders.

At her fourth request he found himself somewhat tired, raw. A distant rooster crowed. He glanced nervously at the sky lightening in the east. What time was it? What if some early rising farmer stumbled past? Wouldn't her family notice she was missing? He felt glad at last when he was able to finish and pull on his breeches. He listened in the darkness as she quickly dressed. He heard her rustling through the grass, folding the blanket, tidying up as if she were a proper housewife. And still she did not speak.

He felt her suddenly take his arm. With hot breath she whispered into his ear, "I will let you know when to come again." And like that she was gone. She didn't say how she'd get home or which way she came. She simply vanished through the woods.

Will, sensing that he should not follow her, waited until he could no longer hear her movements. He pressed his cupped hand to his nose and inhaled. *Violets.*

Chapter Fourteen

Now that they'd parted and Will was certain he wouldn't be caught, he felt strangely alive. Every cricket's chirp, every resonating sheep's bleat, sounded like music. The brightening sky bruised purple—a color he'd never noticed before—and the dark, shapeless fields began to lighten and sharpen into rows of ripening oats and barley. Smells shifted, now fetid as cow muck, now pungent as the damp fur of a newborn kitten, now sweet as wild roses. He felt intoxicated by the fullness, the shimmer of dawn.

No one had seen. Nothing could touch him. This woman was certainly different from all the others he'd ever known. She enjoyed lovemaking in a way that was both startling and a little frightening. He didn't like to admit this. She was older, true. He ran his hand through his hair and paused to consider this lunacy, this wild notion. A proper yeoman's daughter—not a drab, giglot, or wench—who took such pleasure in him. Perhaps he was more marvelous than he'd ever considered.

And yet, here he was, one in a million—a billion perhaps—who had the ample joy and pleasure of relations with a woman who knew what she wanted. Who seemed to ask nothing in return. This realization made him feel bolder than ever. Clearly, she wanted and desired his marvelous self. Perhaps he'd awakened something in her. Perhaps what happened was all his doing, his artistry, his skill. She was practically a spinster. Twenty-eight, wasn't it? Ancient, really. She should have been glad he'd come, glad he'd been so good to her.

The rest of the way home he considered this remarkable, flattering idea. And he wondered when she'd meet with him again. *Four times,* he told himself. *Now there's something!*

He soared up Rother Street, past shadows and alleyways, past darkened windows and bolted doors; he didn't notice anyone spying on him. He'd come home just before dawn before. Why should this return have looked any different?

Stealthily he climbed up the tree, opened the broken shutter, and slipped inside the window. He tiptoed around the sleeping forms of his brothers on pallets strewn on the floor, found his own bed, and fell asleep.

When he awoke, he felt strangely pleased with

himself. He looked on the floor beside his pallet, half-expecting to find the folded wings he'd taken off and discarded. How else had he sailed to such heights?

Carefully he tiptoed around his sleeping brothers to the table with a pitcher and cup. He drank some water to rinse his mouth. When he glanced in the mirror, he admired his stubbly chin. Then he noticed a small purplish mark on his neck, shaped like a woman's mouth. That was when he remembered the night before. He had not imagined it. He had really met her in the field by Two Elms. He smiled, recalling the delights. What a remarkable lover he'd become!

He removed his doublet and discovered the sonnets he'd tucked there and forgotten. The sight was as startling as finding the providential *A* and *W* on the back of his breeches. Anne, the chaste and pure love of his life! He opened the pages and reread one of the poems, which he found most wonderful.

How, he wondered, had he ever found himself in that field last night? How could he have so easily betrayed his sweet and pure Anne of Temple Grafton? A momentary transgression, he told himself. Nothing more. It would, he vowed, never happen again.

As soon as he folded the pages, he caught a whiff of violets. Somehow the scent of Anne of Shottery had rubbed itself insidiously into his clothing, his skin, *and* his sonnets. This, he knew, would never do. He intended to deliver the sonnets this very morning.

The sudden confluence of these two very different Annes disturbed him. He frowned, thinking of the disaster if they should ever meet. The one, whom he loved, and the other, for whom he lusted. Well, there was a simple solution to this problem. He found fresh paper under his pallet and recopied the poems.

Inspired by his guilt, he added a fourth:

Those lines that I before have writ do lie,
Even those that said I could not love you dearer.
Yet then my judgement knew no reason why
My most full flame should afterwards burn clearer.
But reckoning Time, whose million'd accidents
Creep in 'twixt vows, and change decrees of kings,
'Tan sacred beauty, blunt the sharp'st intents,
Divert strong minds to the course of altering things;
Alas, why, fearing of Time's tyranny,
Might I not then say, "Now I love you best,"
When I was certain o'er uncertainty,
Crowning the present, doubting of the rest?
*   Love is a babe; then might I not say so,*
*   To give full growth to that which still doth grow.*

Will reread the last lines because they pleased him so much. This was, he thought, the best thing he'd ever written. And he owed it all to Anne Whateley— so chaste, so delightfully innocent, so absolutely unattainable. His desire to woo her made him feverish. The other Anne, the Anne of stolen pleasures, was only practice, a tutor for his love. She made him burn, true. But this other Anne, now here was the prize. Anyone could see she was a maiden of virtue.

Will folded the poems and replaced them inside his doublet. With these sonnets surely he would win Anne, chaste Anne, good Anne. He would go to her and tell her his true heart. He would be the one to change her mind.

As for Richard, well, what could he do? He was three days' horse ride away in London. By the time he managed to return, he'd realize the hopelessness of his situation, wouldn't he? Will was better suited to his Anne than Richard. She read Ovid and appreciated true poetry. *And I am a poet.*

Will smiled and climbed two steps at a time down the stairway to the hearth. A smoky fire burned in the fireplace. As soon as his mother saw him, she unceremoniously handed him a sloshing jordan. "Dump it, will you, Will?"

Suddenly his dreams of glory and triumphant love dimmed.

That afternoon was his first opportunity to escape from the shop. He raced to Temple Grafton to deliver his masterpiece and confess to Anne that he was the one who'd written the verses. But Anne was not at home when he arrived, and he reluctantly left his poetry with her sister. When he came back the next day with more sonnets, again the story was the same. "Anne is not here," her sister said, and smiled.

"She's not gone to France has she?" Will asked nervously.

Her sister smiled in a way he found most irritating. "Not yet."

"I'll come tomorrow, then," Will said.

"Tomorrow's Sabbath," her sister reminded him.

What else could he do but leave the sonnet folded and sealed? He did not dare to offend Anne by interrupting her prayers. Beyond a doubt she was the most pious young woman he'd ever met.

Two days left, he thought miserably as he headed for home. There were only two days until the arrival of August. His whole life seemed to hang in the balance. He did not know if he could live until he saw her again.

As luck would have it, Father kept an especially sharp eye on him and did not allow him to sneak away from the shop all day on Monday. An excuse to go to Temple Grafton did not arise until Tuesday morning. Under the desperate pretext of making a delivery to Luddington, Will managed to escape from the shop that morning. He rushed to Temple Grafton filled with expectation and dread. *August first!* What if he was too late?

He was so preoccupied with disaster that at first he was unaware that it was Lammas Day, the Gule of August. On this day the first loaves of bread were baked from the first ripe ears of wheat. Since it had been a good season, the harvest was expected to be plentiful. Ripe ears of wheat hung over the doorways of the out-of-the-way churches. Once, long, long ago, landowners had brought lambs to sacrifice at church. Now the people offered loaves of bread on the altars. Even this custom was not highly regarded by the churchmen, who believed in thanksgiving services only after times of difficulty—not to celebrate such idols as "corn babies" made from first sheaves and other pagan rites.

Will passed fields filled with reapers, who moved through the grain with scythes and sang:

"Now Lammas comes in
Our harvest begins.
We have now to endeavor to get the corn in.
We reap and we mow,
And stoutly we blow
And cut down the corn that sweetly did grow."

The song gave him hope. Maybe delivering his poetry on Lammas Day would bring him luck.

When he finally arrived at Anne's house at Temple Grafton, he was surprised to see a horse tied outside. *Odd.* Was it a visitor come to celebrate Lammas with Anne's family?

Boldly Will knocked on the door. The door swung open and there stood Anne, looking just as fair and lovely as Will had remembered. When she smiled at him, he was dazzled as if by blinding light. He was just about to greet her when he heard a startling voice call to him from within, "Hello, Cousin."

Richard!

There at Anne's table with a tankard of Anne's father's ale and a plate of onions and cheese prepared by Anne's sister sat Will's friend wearing a handsome new green doublet.

The sight was more than Will could bear. He

shuffled through the doorway filled with sorrow and defeat. "Good morrow, Richard," he mumbled. "When did you arrive from London?"

"Yesterday," Richard said. He strode across the room and clasped Will in a choking bear hug. "Today is the first of August."

"Yes," said Will uncertainly. Then he glanced at Anne, whose eyes beamed with happiness. Suddenly Will felt a cold rush of fear. *August first.* Something had happened. Something about Anne's decision. "Richard," Will asked in an urgent voice, "may I speak to you alone?"

"Of course," said Richard in a bright voice that Will found unnerving. "We won't be gone long, Anne." He followed Will outside.

"What are you doing here?" Will demanded.

"Perhaps I should ask the same of you," said Richard in a jovial, grating voice. "The truth is that I am glad you are here for my support. Today I formally ask Anne to be my wife."

"Your wife?" Will gulped. This news was far worse than Will had imagined. For a moment, he could not breathe.

"Speak, man!" Richard said, and laughed. "I intend to make so convincing a case that I sweep her off her feet."

"But what of France? What of her going away?"

"I'm sure that will be a subject soon discarded forever," Richard said in a low, confiding voice.

"But you are . . . you are so young. And she is only seventeen. Why not enjoy your freedom longer? Besides, your apprenticeship forbids marriage. You will give up good employment in London for her?"

Richard laughed. "Certainly not."

Will felt even more confused. "Then what are you doing?"

Richard smiled. "My job in London goes surprisingly well. My master is so pleased, I have been promoted. I've come to make my fortunes known and to ask officially for Anne's hand. What is a wait of two or three years?"

Will remained too stunned to speak.

"Your poetry has worked wonders," Richard continued. "You must stay while I press my proposal. You are my good luck charm. I will not take no for an answer."

Will gritted his teeth. "I have a special sonnet that I came to deliver."

"Excellent!" said Richard.

Something writhed in Will's stomach. He knew he had no future. There was nothing about his present circumstances that made his prospects look the least bit promising. Richard was the suitor with the ambition, the promotion, the talent, and the new green doublet. What did he have? Nothing.

Glumly he followed Richard back into the house. Anne sat demurely at the table with needlework in her lap. Neither her sister nor parents were anywhere in sight. When she looked up at Will with her clear blue eyes, he felt as if she were capable of seeing all his secrets, all his faults, his sins from the night nearly a week ago. He thought he might die.

Richard stooped near her ear and whispered something. She smiled. Richard's familiarity made Will furious. He had a sudden urge to rush at Richard, push him aside, then force him outdoors, where he'd shove him face-first into the dirt with his arm twisted behind his back.

And yet, Will could do none of these things. He could not even speak.

"What's wrong with you? Are you ill?" Richard asked. Again that perverse smile. That slack-jawed grin. Why had Will never noticed before how much Richard reminded him of a donkey? He could hardly bear to see Richard standing there trying to converse with her. They were undoubtedly talking about him. Laughing. See how he chuckled under his breath and then glanced his way?

Will couldn't look at her. What if she smiled? What if she was sharing Richard's cruel joke? Will shot her a quick glance. She wasn't smiling. *Good.* Her face was set and stolid as fine marble. Her blessed perfection.

"Good morrow, Will," she said. Her voice rang with the musical lilt of thrushes in early morning or the call of doves in spring. In her pale left hand he caught a glimpse of a rosary wound around her delicate wrist. Rosaries were forbidden, and yet there she was holding one in daylight where anyone could see. It was a sign, he decided. She trusted them to keep her secret.

"Good morrow, Anne," Will said in a bashful voice. See how she smiled? She was his refuge, his haven.

"That's all you have to say?" Richard laughed his hee-haw laugh.

Will tugged off his cap and twisted it nervously. Her gaze seemed to go through him like strong summer light through the leaves of a lily, revealing all veins and lines, all places chewed away by bugs or the nibbling of water rats.

"Anne says you have been most dutiful in bringing the poems as I requested," Richard said in a pleased voice, all the while keeping his donkey gaze focused on Anne. "Anne, how did you find them?"

Her eyelashes fluttered shut for a moment. Will felt as if he'd never witnessed such startling joy.

"They were indeed the most beautiful things I ever read," she said and glanced at Will. In that moment, he felt as if all the air was squeezed from his lungs.

"And how does your father take my offer?" Richard continued eagerly.

Will clenched his fists. *What a knave!* He'd kill him right here, right now, if Anne weren't present.

"I have not heard him say anything yet," Anne said slowly. She adjusted the dark beads of the rosary against her wrist. "You know my feelings on this matter."

"Yes, yes," Richard replied with some impatience. "You are so young—"

"I know my mind," she interrupted.

Will's heart gave a leap of hope.

"I have always wanted to go to the convent. Now that there is no other place so holy left in England, I must go to France to seek shelter. These are dangerous times for believers in the Old Faith."

Will hunched forward, too stunned at first to imagine the enormity of this disaster. *The convent! My life is ruined.* How could he have been so cursed as to fall in love with a chaste woman of his parents' faith?

"Now, now, Anne—" Richard said.

"My vocation as a nun," she continued, "is the only way I can make my way and serve the Lord."

"We have time," Richard said, his voice moving slightly from eager brightness to something harder, more unbending. "You and I have several years to be betrothed. Then my apprenticeship will be finished. I will have a good job in London. My master says he likes my work. He says he might eventually make me a partner in his shop."

Will felt as if he was going to be sick. Going to France to be a nun? *Who put such an awful notion in her mind?* He'd like to throttle that person. And yet any fool could see she was serious. Now who would save him? Who would redeem him?

Suddenly he had a vision of her beauty, her youth fading away in a distant French convent—a damp, airless stone building. He couldn't help but imagine her crimson cheeks turned pale as forest mushrooms, her lips pinched, brow wrinkled, eyes scowling. Little by little, all youthful vigor shrunken and shriveled like a flower picked too soon and discarded. "No!" Will blurted out. "Anne, you cannot."

Anne and Richard looked at him with surprise, as if they'd forgotten he was even standing there. "Cannot what?" Anne said in a soft voice.

"Give yourself up to the convent," Will said. He spoke so quickly and with such feeling that his hands flew about like crazed birds.

"That is for God to decide," Anne replied. She unwound then wound the rosary around her wrist.

"And what of your father's wishes?" Richard said. "He has told me that he seeks a husband for you and that he will offer a handsome parcel of land in dowry. He told me—"

"I seek obedience to something higher," Anne said.

Richard's mouth snapped shut. He looked stunned.

His friend's momentary retreat gave Will courage. "Anne, you will," he said slowly, "accept one last poem? I came here to deliver this."

Richard smiled gratefully at Will, as if never suspecting anything.

Will cleared his throat and read the poem he wrote as a kind of confession, his declaration of love:

"Will will fulfill the treasure of thy love."

Will paused. He could see Richard glaring at him now. But he continued:

"For nothing hold me, so it please thee hold
That nothing me, a something, sweet, to thee—"

"That's quite enough," Richard grumbled. "Hand me that paper."

"Let him finish," Anne said. She sat and gave Will her rapt attention.

Encouraged, Will added some energy to his reading for full effect:

*"Make but my name thy love, and love that still,
And then thou lovest me, for my name is* Will."

He held the quivering poem in his hand and looked at Anne. She dabbed a tear from her eye with her apron hem.

"You snake!" Richard shouted. "All the time I had you coming here delivering your sonnets, you were wooing her right under my nose."

"You were in London," Will said. He peeked at Anne, who glanced at Richard in shock. "You told me to write them and deliver them. I was only doing what you said."

"You mean the sonnets weren't yours, Richard?" Anne demanded.

Richard blushed, caught in his own trap. A muscle in his jaw quivered. "He was supposed to help me. He was supposed to plead my case—not his own."

"You lied," Anne said in a prim voice. "You lied to me."

Richard sighed. "Will you forgive me?"

Anne bowed her head. "Perhaps. But I will never marry you, Richard. Not after this."

Richard turned on his heel. He plucked Will by his arm and dragged him out into the yard. With little ceremony he pulled off his new green doublet, threw it over a fence post, and rolled up his sleeves. "Knave! Scoundrel!" he shouted at Will.

Likewise, Will stripped to his fighting mode. He knew his friend well enough to feint to the right; his powerful uppercut had nearly cost him a broken nose on several occasions. Will bounced to the left, to the right. He held his arms up in fists and moved about the yard.

"Please, please stop!" Anne cried. She stood in the doorway looking fearful and fascinated at the same time. Seeing her pale, Christian image out of the corner of his eye had an odd effect on Will. Instead of butting Richard in the stomach with his head—the way that always brought him down quickly—Will did nothing.

Richard swung. His punch landed squarely against Will's jaw. Blood spurted. Anne screamed. Will staggered backward. Richard slugged him again. Will didn't react. He bent double and sprawled in the dirt.

"Stop! Stop!" Anne screamed. She rushed toward them, hovering over Will like an angel of mercy. He blubbered incoherently that he loved her. Overhead, he saw the furious face of his best friend, now his worst enemy. Richard's bright red face wavered and wobbled. Now another face. A man Will didn't know. "Are you all right?" the fellow asked, then Anne's voice crying, "Richard, look at what you've done. You could have killed him." Will could feel something tender like a woman's hands dabbing his forehead. "Go away!" she said. Her voice a chant, an incantation. "Never come back here!"

Will closed his eyes, victorious.

Chapter Fifteen

Days passed and Will heard no word from Richard, who'd departed for London in great haste after their fight. Slowly, summer's light began to fade. Shocks of grain stood in the fields. Apples ripened in the orchards. Geese were plucked. During festivities to celebrate the harvest a garland of flowers crowned the captain of the reapers, and it was a merry time of good cheer and feasting, for there seemed to be plenty of barley, oats, and rye and for once no one spoke of a hungry winter.

For Will, too, life seemed to hold infinite promise. Every available moment he spent in Temple Grafton, where he listened to the illicit prayers and forbidden sermons of chaste, beatific Anne. She never mentioned the French convent again. Instead, she seemed to have taken on Will as her project for salvation. Their meetings to study the lives of saints were thrillingly secret and dangerous. If they were caught, they'd be imprisoned.

Yet Will felt the risk was worth it. He'd impressed Anne's aging father so ably with his pious behavior and thoughtful gifts of fresh-picked apples and pints of honey that he was allowed free access to Anne's home. In fact, Anne's father seemed to look forward to Will's visits.

"Here's William," her father called to Anne one unseasonably warm September afternoon. As usual, Anne was in prayer when Will arrived. "How are you, William? How is your father's business?"

"Very well, sir," Will replied, as if he were a gentleman born—not the son of a marked man wanted for debt and stubborn connection to the Old Faith.

Dutifully Anne worked with Will to perfect his lapses in reciting the catechism—never once suspecting that her father saw Will as his headstrong daughter's salvation. "Anything," he once confided in Will, "is better than the nunnery far away in France."

Anne and Will sat outside her house as the sun began to set. "We ought diligently to search our heart to the bottom," Anne said with great conviction. "Deeply consider the paths we tread in. Walk warily, lest hereafter we say with sorrowful spirit: 'Oh that I had considered the end as well as the beginning of my actions; then should I have increased in favor with God and man.'"

Will heard none of her words. He was too busy observing the motion of her lovely, forbidden lips. He tried to keep unruly passions from his heart, even though he felt a kind of guilty pleasure in taking over his friend's place as Anne's wooer.

Anne performed her job nobly. With diligence she refused to allow Will to touch her hand or kiss her cheek.

Will thought he might go mad.

Later that evening when Will returned home, Whittington delivered a second secret message from Shottery. Will tried not to feel excited with anticipation. He spent the time waiting reading the Bible. He rehearsed his speech: how he'd heard a higher calling, how he could not jeopardize his holy vows or new religious zeal. And yet as soon as the cathedral bell struck midnight, he climbed out his chamber window and sprinted to meet Anne Hathaway behind a deserted barn near Salmon Trail. The moment she touched him, he forgot his pious words. He forgot the danger of being caught. He forgot everything except the smell of violets and the sensation of high, wide soaring.

And so Will began his double existence. By day he spent his few free hours in Temple Grafton with lovely Anne, who tutored him with pure, impossible speeches. By night he stole away to an abandoned weaver's cottage on the road to Evesham to meet with Anne of Shottery. She always selected the place. She always informed him of their next meeting through Whittington, who did not read and only delivered instructions folded and sealed—sometimes at the shop, other times on the street when he spied Will and followed him on foot.

At first Will found visits from the dirty shepherd vaguely disturbing. Old Whittington never spoke, never even said hello. Soon, however, Will began to expect him. He even found himself searching for Whittington's slouching figure up Chapel Street or at the Rother Market.

Once Will tried to speak to Whittington. "Good-day," he mumbled.

The loyal shepherd would have no conversation. He simply waved his gnarled hand, handed him the message, and departed. Will wondered what Whittington thought of these deliveries for his mistress. Was he as mute and unknowing as he seemed?

And yet Will convinced himself that Anne knew what she was doing—the same way he trusted that she would not become with child. She hinted she had her own methods—a special hot drink made of a mixture of spices and the juice of the herb savin. She refused to say much more than that. Will trusted her because she was older and seemed so confident and experienced. Everyone in town knew that after her father's death, motherless Anne had acquired a pleasing inheritance. More money was promised in her father's will after she married.

"I am," she had once proudly whispered to Will, "wholly at my own government." This both thrilled and confused Will, who did not know whether to be flattered or belittled by her obvious economic superiority. "I can finally do as I wish," she said, "and no mother, no father, no brother, can stop me."

The urgency of her secret daring enthralled Will. He was delighted that she did not speak of love or marriage or any other annoyance or binding contract. Unlike all the other young women he knew, Anne of Shottery seemed not to care about such things. This suited Will perfectly. Their clandestine meetings occurred quickly, quietly, and ably, in order to avoid detection by neighbors.

"I must begone now. Farewell," she said in a low voice one late September evening under a full moon.

"Jesu, what haste! Can you not stay awhile?" Will leaned back and stared at the stars. "Do you know in all these weeks we have scarcely spoken more than a few sentences to each other?"

"What is there to say?" Anne replied, and slipped back on her skirt.

Will linked his fingers behind his head and lifted his neck slightly to study her mysterious silhouette. "How do you spend your days?"

"Why do you wish to know?"

Will sighed and rested his head again on the ground. "I am only trying to imagine how you lead your life. I know you can write. I assume you can read. I was wondering if you enjoy poetry or—"

"My days are long and dull," she interrupted. "My stepmother is a lean-witted fool. My father's land barely provides enough to support her children—five detestable parasites. And that is why I oversee the work of the house servants and farm laborers. I keep accounts of the kitchen stores. Like a proper maid, I can do needlework. I can spin. How I spend my evenings is my own business."

" 'Between the acres of the rye,' " Will sang softly. " 'With a hey, and a ho, and a hey nonino—' "

"Hush!" she hissed. "Do you wish to wake the world?"

"I am only trying to cheer you, proper maid," he

replied, delighted to think that she, too, led a kind of double life. "What gives you pleasure?"

"Are you trying to be cruel?"

"No," Will said, barely able to conceal his disappointment. He had hoped she would describe his visits as her only true delight. "I am curious about you, that's all. As I said, we so seldom have any conversation."

"You don't come for conversation, do you?"

Will remained silent for a moment. Her spiteful tone made him feel uneasy. He wished for once he could see the expression on her face. Her moods seemed as fathomless as the night's darkness. "Until tomorrow, then?" he said in a hopeful voice.

"Perhaps," she replied, and hurried out of sight.

The next day at noon Will decided to change his routine and wandered into the Swan for a tankard of ale and a bite to eat. The hares were fat, some poachers told him, and it had been a decent season for stolen harts as well. If Richard were here, they'd have a good hunt. For the first time, Will missed the company of Richard, the one person who understood him completely. The one person who would listen to his problems. He wondered what Richard was doing and how he was faring. He had not heard anything from anyone about Richard. Suddenly Will had the notion of making amends and reconciling—if only he could find a way to do it.

No woman, Will decided, was worth this kind of loneliness.

He took a seat and pulled a piece of paper from his doublet. Dully, he unfolded the blank page. In spite of constant romantic daring and intrigue, his life seemed as empty as this sheet. *"You should do what gives you passion."* Wasn't that what that strange little man had told him? Will's encounter with the theater company in June seemed so long ago, he wondered if the experience had only been a dream. Last week during an errand for Father, Will had stopped on the street to listen to some distant jingling and shouting—signs that the players might be returning. When he discovered that the noises were nothing more than the jangling of a mule's harness and the bellowing of the animal's driver, he felt stung with disappointment. *Maybe they're never coming back.*

To try to amuse himself, he'd made it his routine during his respite from his father's shop to hide in the tavern and write a sonnet or two. He enjoyed the escape, and Anne of Temple Grafton seemed to appreciate the verses as long as they weren't "too sensuous or overfilled with ardor." It was a challenge to write something that fit her pious literary demands. He often didn't like what he wrote, because the verses seemed so weak, so vapid compared with what he truly felt. Just as he was about to begin writing some insipid poem about God's love, a familiar voice called out to him.

"Hello, Will." Mopsa stood beside him watching him work. In her strong hands she held full tankards for the next table. "You've been avoiding me for almost three months."

She sounded deeply hurt, yet Will did not bother to look up from his paper. "Hmmmmph," he replied. The last thing he wanted right now was for jealous Mopsa to berate him for neglecting her.

"Have you been up the High Cross way? There's a poor woman in the stocks they say. She's with child and she's got no husband, and I don't see that's fair for her to be punished and the man to go free. When winter comes, who'll feed the babe if it lives?"

Annoyed, Will hunched lower and kept scribbling.

"Can't even find no place for her to sleep, since it's against the law to harbor a pregnant woman who's unmarried." Mopsa's voice was hurried and insistent, and she spoke far too loudly. "These are hard, cold times for the unfortunates. Not like you who's got everything he needs. Maybe more than he needs."

Will shrugged, uncertain of her meaning. He glanced about the room and hoped that no one was listening.

"Ale, wench!" a man at the next table shouted.

"Must be going, Will. You take care of yourself. You look haggard and wore. You get any sleep at all?" she said, then added in a low voice, "There's them that watches all comings and goings."

"Hmmmmmmph," said Will. He quickly finished one last line, then glanced up at her with feigned interest. "After work today, then?"

"I'm busy," she said, and gave him a sorrowful look. "Good-bye, Will."

"Wench, bring us that ale!"

"Good-bye?" Will replied, then tried to make a joke of her farewell. "I'll see you after work, I will."

Mopsa sighed. With sudden tenderness she briefly touched the back of his head with her rough hand. "You won't, Will," she said, then turned away. "You know you won't."

Will nodded and nibbled the end of the quill. She was right. Quite right. He wouldn't.

By the middle of October, lofty winds stripped the trees of the last leaves. Hogs grew fat on fallen acorns in the forest. Basket makers scoured the woods for rods. Fishermen set up great nets in the river.

While everyone in town had nearly forgotten the great slandering of the bishop, Whitgift himself proved to have a very long memory indeed. There was nothing so abhorrent to the proud cleric as an insult from a recusant.

One late afternoon in the glowering darkness, Will trudged home from Temple Grafton with his cloak held tightly to protect himself from the sharp wind. *What's this?* He paused in surprise. An unusually large, boisterous crowd had gathered on Henley Street. Such a sight meant that the town crier must be about to announce one of two possible things: another excommunication or a hanging.

Without warning, Will's stomach lurched. Up until this moment, he'd never considered the obvious, the inescapable. What if someone accused him of participation in the crime of fornication? *Impossible.* He tried to reassure himself that there were no witnesses. And yet he felt his face grow strangely hot while thinking of his double life. If Anne of Shottery found herself with child, he'd be no better than Thomas Burman, stripped of his credit and name, and humiliated publicly in church dressed in nothing but a white sheet. And what would Anne of Temple Grafton think of him then? Will wiped the sweat from his upper lip. The sorrows and accusations heaped upon him would be worse than anything he could bear.

"Will? You deaf?" his father boomed from across the milling crowd. "Get inside. We need help."

Will darted through the throng and rushed in the door, thankful to be safe and warm. His back suddenly ached at the shoulder blades.

"You ill?" his father demanded.

"No," Will said wearily.

"Feeling tired, dear heart?" said Joan, who carried a load of wet laundry to the garden. She paused to glance critically at him over the wet, wrung-out bundles.

"I'm fine," Will replied in an angry voice.

"Perhaps if you slept at night, you'd be better off. Your humors would not be so out of sorts."

"Leave me be," he grumbled.

"Burning a candle at both ends. I think that's what they call it." She smiled sweetly. "Be careful you don't get burned."

Will growled at her to be on her way. The thought of the hangman's noose, white sheets, and public confessions had made him edgy. Why couldn't people leave him alone? Why did Mopsa, Joan, his father, and everyone else have to stick their noses into his business? All secrets known. All desires spoken. There was nowhere to hide in this town.

Suddenly the little man's face and voice came unbidden. *"Have you ever traveled?"*

Will gulped. In London no one would question him about his every move, his every thought. He'd be free. *Should have run away when I had the chance.*

The back door banged shut. When Will peered out through the shutter, he noticed that the crowd was getting bigger. He recognized neighbors. Others seemed to be strangers—perhaps from the next parish. "What's going on out there, Father?" he asked in a low voice.

"Don't like the look of it," Father replied, and unfolded a piece of hide at his worktable. "Look busy. Act innocent."

Will felt too nervous to go back to work. He peeked out again. Women bundled in dark woolen shawls held their baskets and bags close to their bodies and tried to tiptoe to see over the shoulders of taller men. Children dashed in and out between legs, their faces eager and red with the possibility of calamity. A dog barked.

"The constable," Will whispered.

"What's he doing?" said Father.

"He's coming this way."

There was a heavy, official rapping at the door. "What should I do?" Will asked anxiously.

"Open the door. Let me do the talking," said Father.

Will did as he was told. The constable removed his hat and stepped through the doorway. In spite of the wind and cold, Father signaled to Will to keep the door open wide. The crowd pushed closer so that they could see and hear what was going on inside the shop.

A feckless child flipped a small pebble in the air and let it fall on the floor near Will's foot. Will shot him a fierce look, and the boy darted out of sight.

"I wish a word with your son," the constable told Father.

Father's face turned red, yet his expression seemed inscrutable. "The constable wishes a word with you," Father announced. Father used what Will called his bailiff voice, the voice Father employed when he was cornered by officials. It was the voice Father used when he seemed to wish to appear powerful and wise—a voice from the old days when he'd been high bailiff, the most commanding figure in the town.

The constable tucked his arms around his stout body and glowered, so that his unruly eyebrows met at his forehead like one long, angry caterpillar. "You know anything about a straw dummy meant to slander the good name of our bishop this past summer on Thursday, the twenty-sixth of July?"

"Straw dummy?" Will gulped. The crowd murmured recklessly. He felt all their eyes upon him. "No, sir."

The constable coughed and wiped his nose with his sleeve. He was ordinarily the baker, one of Father's drinking comrades. His job as constable was a weary, onerous task that had been passed among the respectable merchants in town. It was a three-month stint that could not be refused but was never welcomed by anyone.

The baker-turned-constable motioned for the crowd to step back with the same kind of impatience he used to break up a mob waiting for freshly baked bread. "There is some who say you had something to do with it, Will. You can land yourself in the jail for such rough talk against church officials." He lowered his voice and then shot a glance in Father's direction. "Don't need to tell you these is dangerous times to talk against religion. We got your brother in the stocks."

"Hal?" Father said slowly. "What are the charges?"

"Drunkenness, scandal mongering, personal abuse, and defamation. He was shouting and swearing great profanities."

"He's raving again," Father said quickly. "You know how drink affects his dim brain."

"Aye," the constable said, "but this is perilous slander even for a drunk man."

Father nodded. Will felt a terrible chill overtake

him, and he shivered. What had his uncle said? Will's mind was empty of any words, any reasonable excuse that might save him. The crowd pressed closer, as if eager for some sign of guilt. Someone swung open the shutter for a better view. No one liked Whitgift or his band of spies. Yet it seemed to thrill the throng to have one among them pay the price for their own hateful thoughts.

"I didn't do anything meant disrespectful, sir," Will murmured. He kept his eyes lowered. It had happened so long ago, he thought everybody had forgotten.

"He's a young, wild boy still, Constable," Will's father said. "Like all of us when we was that age, he done his own share of troubles. Why don't you let me take care of his punishment, since I'm his father? I'll beat the daylights out of him, I promise you, whether he's guilty or not."

The crowd broke into a clatter of confused voices. A private beating was certainly not as entertaining as a public flogging and a branding up at High Cross.

"I don't know now, John," the constable said to Father in hushed tones. It was clear he was considering the idea.

"We've been through much together," Father continued quietly. He leveled a frank, open gaze at his friend as if to remind him of pots of small ale and cups of sack shared, baptisms celebrated, late-night jokes at Attwood's. "You must certainly recall that incident with the summons and your sister. How I dismissed the charges against her for making charms and helps for people and cattle."

The constable squirmed. Clearly he didn't enjoy the idea of punishing the son of the former high bailiff, his friend and neighbor, who had protected his family against the dangerous declarations of sorcery.

"Let me see to his punishment," said Father. "You can stand right here on the street and witness his distress. I mean to beat him with all the harshness I can muster. And you know I'm a man of my word, don't you?"

The constable was silent, deep in thought. Then he rubbed his chin and jerked a thumb toward the shop. "I'll leave it to you. We can't have folks making fun of the bishop. Whether your son was involved or not, I need to show we took some action. Whitgift's an impatient man. He's had to wait months to see justice done. Will's still a minor and your apprentice. I'll let you handle it this once. But if ever again I find you involved in such disreputable behavior, Will," he said in an ominous voice, "you'll not be spared. Do you understand me?"

The constable stepped outside and waved at the

crowd. "Move back. Give a man some space. The boy's being beat by his father."

The crowd booed. Will's face burned. He made a small bow in the direction of the constable. Father gave Will a rough push past his mother, who sobbed into her apron. Will trudged past his terrified brothers and sister. "Upstairs!" Father barked at Will. "The rest of you go to your business." His brothers and sister fled. Father followed Will to the chamber above the shop. He opened wide the chamber window. Biting wind blew inside.

"Get along now," the constable bellowed at the crowd. Of course, no one intended to go anywhere until they had heard Will's cries with their own ears.

Father locked the chamber door. Then he took down the long leather belt he kept hooked to the wall behind the door. Father had not punished Will with the strap since he was ten and made off with Widow Crump's pastry, cooling on her windowsill.

Father kept his angry expression even as he motioned silently for Will to stand out of the way. Will looked at him in surprise. His father used a kind of crude sign language to direct Will to slide the straw pallet to the center of the room. Clearly he intended to wallop the pallet, not Will. Will's role in the scene was to howl as loudly as he could. When Will realized his father's intentions, he felt an enormous sense of relief. He wasn't going to be punished after all.

Whump! The strap hit the pallet.

In his best theatrical voice Will let out a blood-curdling yell. His father hit the pallet again. *Whump!*

Will yowled pitifully.

Will and his father playacted for a good twenty wallops while the crowd below cheered. When Father finished, Will stayed up in the chamber sniveling loudly while his father clumped noisily down to the street to confirm for the constable what everyone in the neighborhood had heard. His son was dutifully punished, and justice had been served.

When Father returned to the house, he pushed roughly past his wife at the bottom of the stairs. "How bad is he bleeding?" she demanded. "You didn't beat him about the face, did you? You didn't scar him, did you?"

Father did not answer. He stomped up the steps to the upper chamber above the shop. His furious expression took Will aback. "I will tell you for the last time. My brother's the most untrustworthy knave in Christendom," his father whispered. "Do not keep company with him. Do not trust him. Do I make myself heard? The next time you may not be so lucky to have me for your hangman."

Will lowered himself onto the pallet. Stunned, he drew his knees close to his chest. His father's words plunged into his back as sharp as a leather strap. Now Will knew for certain.

Uncle Hal had betrayed him.

Chapter Sixteen

October drew to a close, and steady rains began. Dreary drizzle spattered bare tree branches and filled old furrows with cold puddles. Country people came to Rother Market wet and smelling of damp, sour wool. With great effort they pushed their carts, wheels caked in mud and pitifully moiled. With each passing day, sunlight waned. Everyone—from town and farm alike—watched with apprehension as the darkness increased. They knew deep-down, without being told, that soon would come the moment of the sun's yearly death. October thirty-first, All Hallows' Eve, was the last night of the season of the sun. November first heralded the start of the season of darkness and cold.

Before Will's father's father's father was born, Warwickshiremen had burned huge effigies made of wicker and shaped like giants atop the hills on All

Hallows' Eve. No one remembered why exactly. Some said the light helped lost souls find their way. On All Hallows' Eve spirits floated freely, ghosts were said to sit on every stile, and fortune-tellers' words were most likely to come true.

While Bishop Whitgift and other clerics in pulpits outlawed these rites as ancient superstitions, their congregations ignored them and stealthily lit bonfires. Some decorated grave sites with candles and gifts of special food and drink.

On All Hallows' Eve no one wandered beyond the town's walls. It wasn't safe to travel on lonesome country roads after sunset, when so many witches and elves were said to roam. In the darkness a sudden gust of wind blew open the shop door. Will stepped outside to struggle with the latch. Empty Henley Street seemed as silent as a graveyard. *Soon my youth, my ambition will be dead, too.* Will thought of the little man and the theater company and regretted once again his missed opportunity. *I should have escaped this place when I had the chance.*

In the open doorway he looked up at the full moon rising over Price Cox's place across the street. *What will become of me?* His uncle's betrayal, the loss of his best friend, and the exhausting confusion of his love life vexed him. How could he be Lover Not

Loved to Anne of Temple Grafton while at the same time act the part of Loved Not Loving to Anne of Shottery?

In desperation he recalled another moonlit night and a question asked in dangerous darkness. *"Thy fate, dost thou wish to know it?"* Suddenly he yearned to speak to the hag at Charlecote. Such prophets should be taken seriously, especially on a night like this. He had to know his future. What better time than All Hallows' Eve to find her? There wouldn't be another chance for a whole year.

Miraculously his sadness vanished. The daredevil nature of his plan made him feel wonderfully alive. Yes, he would go to Charlecote. He would find the hag and ask her to tell him what she knew.

Just to be completely safe, he took an iron crucifix his father kept hidden beneath his workbench. He tucked this into his wallet, which hung from a belt around his waist. The crucifix would ward off evil spirits he might encounter.

Without telling anyone in his family where he was bound, Will removed his cloak from the peg and hurried out the door and down the street. He knew that if he did not act quickly, he might lose his nerve.

On doorsteps sat jack-o'-lanterns carved from

large turnips and illuminated inside with rags dipped in tallow. Their leering grins seemed to mock him. "Fie!" Will said, and gave one of the jack-o'-lanterns a good kick, then hurried on.

Clouds shrouded the moon. Will ducked in and out of shadows, furtive as a hare. He hoped no one lurked in the darkness, watching him. Once he was outside of town, he made great speed up the road along the river.

With only a half-mile to the fording place, a dog jumped out of the underbrush and growled fiercely. Will froze. Then, as slowly as he could, he moved one foot along the ground to see if he might locate a weapon. The dog rumbled again. Will leaned over and picked up a rock. With surprising accuracy he hurled it hard. He heard a high yip, a cry of pain—and the dog plunged into the bushes and vanished.

Will's heart beat in his throat. A dog alone.

A bad sign. A devil perhaps camouflaged as a wild dog. On such a night, such things were possible. He ran as fast as he could the rest of the way to the fording place.

He tried to calm himself as he untied the dilapidated boat that he and Richard had stolen and hidden in the reeds. Using the hidden paddle, he pushed off and glided along in silence. When the boat bumped along the muddy shore, he jumped out and tied the rope securely to a tree limb.

Wind shook the trees. He tried to remember which way he and Richard had come into the woods, which way they'd walked. He couldn't remember anything. *We had been drunk.* How would he ever be able to retrace his steps? He should go home.

He sniffed. Was that faint rotten-egg odor brimstone? He shivered. Somewhere deep in the woods an owl hooted. Clouds that covered the moon parted, and the light seemed almost as bright as day. There between the bare ash trees he could see the path. Bravely, he took a deep breath and walked into the woods.

Just as he remembered, the trees and the light had a strange, dreamlike quality. His feet shuffled through the dry leaves. The sound seemed deafening.

He kept walking. A branch broke. Will gulped. Smoke, he was sure of it. He smelled smoke. Beyond he could see the clearing.

"Why, how now, Will?"

The shrill voice made Will jump. He was breathing very fast, holding so tight to the iron crucifix in his hand, it bit his skin.

"Where hast thou been?"

"Home, madame," he mumbled. His mouth felt too dry to form many words. He stared into the clearing, searching for the wizened shape. Something crackled. Beyond a leafless bush he spied the lick of flame beneath a kettle. "Where are you?"

"Here, sir," called the hag. A dark outline hobbled into view and stood before the fire. She stirred something in the pot. "Hungry art thou?"

Who knew what might be in that kettle? Eye of newt, toe of frog, wool of bat, or tongue of dog. "No, madame, but thank you kindly."

"Thou art fortunate my weird sisters aren't present. They'd insist thou have a taste."

Will felt as if he might gag. "I'm . . . I'm really not the least bit famished, madame." Desperately he hoped she wouldn't think him rude. Nervously he glanced about the clearing. "When will your—your sisters be back?"

"They're out and about. Killing swine, gathering chestnuts, plucking snakes. In a foggy cloud hither and yon. Flying here. Flying there. They never say when they shall return. One of us must stay behind and tend the fire. One of us must remain at home. Not like thou, Will."

"Not me? Pray, tell me more."

"Thou wishest to know thy fate?"

"Does it have to do with leaving home?"

"I'll give thee a wind. In a sieve wilt thou thither sail?"

Will tugged at the choking collar of his cloak. Her words weren't the least bit helpful. Why did she talk in such riddles? "I don't have much time, madame," he said guardedly. "I must get back to—"

She cackled. "Stay and listen," she insisted. "Thou shalt venture on a great journey while never straying farther than thy hearth, though one day thou wilt leave behind what thou lovest best."

"I don't—don't understand," Will stammered. How could he go on a journey and never leave his own hearth? And what did she mean by leaving what he loved best? This wasn't the news he wished to hear. There had to be an explanation. "Tell me more," he begged. "Speak, madame."

She turned away from him, took something from deep inside the grimy folds of her dark dress, and sprinkled it into the fire. A huge cloud of smoke reared up and swallowed her. Will stumbled backward, shielding his eyes. When the smoke cleared, the hag had vanished.

Chapter Seventeen

Will stumbled into town early the next morning, dirty, wet, and disheveled. He must have fallen asleep in the woods, he told himself. He couldn't remember how he'd found his way out of Charlecote or how he crossed the river. The hag and the cauldron, these frightening images must only have been a nightmare. He shivered and brushed away dead leaves from his arms, his hair. His clothing smelled of damp moss, dirt, fusty wood, and something else. Smoke. He shook his head in a kind of wonder and terror.

Aching, tired, and hungry, he trudged past the woodyard. When he looked across the river, he saw a group of people gathered on Clopton Bridge. What were they doing? Young boys peered down into the water with curious, intense expressions. None of them carried fishing poles. *Odd.*

Curious, Will climbed the small hill to the bridge

and stared into the water, too. He saw nothing except roiled water. If anyone else were to observe him at this moment, he wondered, would they notice the strangeness in his eye? Could they tell he'd just spent All Hallows' Eve in the forbidden woods of Charlecote visiting a witch? If anyone found out that he'd consulted such a wicked spirit, he'd be drawn, quartered, and burned at the stake.

The only thing Whitgift loathed more than recusants and overzealous Protestants were witches. Witch hunts were a favorite sport among churchmen, who tied suspected witches at the waist with ropes and tossed them into the millpond. If the suspect didn't sink, she was declared a witch and publicly tortured. In town Goody Thomas was well known as "an ill-look woman," a witch who could cast the evil eye. Once she used her powers on the wife of Adrian Holder and told her to "get her home to hell or I will brush the motes forth of your dirty gown." That was enough to have Goody Thomas promptly reported to the authorities. She was later tortured until she confessed.

No, Will was no fool. He'd keep his mouth shut.

"Over here!" one of the boys shouted, and pointed into the water.

Will leaned over the edge of the bridge and searched the current. He was so busy staring, he didn't hear his sister creep up beside him and rudely give him a poke.

"She's dead you know," Joan said. Her long, greasy hair whipped back from her face. She studied the river with hard eyes.

"Who?" he demanded. Fear ambushed him. *What if the hag made a curse just to spite him?*

"Found her in the river this morning." Joan picked up a rock and hurled it into the black, lapping water.

"Who?" Will repeated, louder this time.

"She told me once how she loved you," she said. Joan's words hit him in the chest.

"Speak the name!" *Not Anne. Please, God, not Anne.*

Joan seemed to find his growing panic perversely amusing. "I can't see why she loved you. The way you treated her."

Will gripped both his sister's arms tight. "Who? Who are you talking about?"

His sister's mouth curled into a cruel smile. Her hooting laughter sounded like a hurt bird or the mournful cry of January wind. "Don't you know? Can't you even guess?"

Will shook her hard. She acted as if she didn't care. She laughed and laughed. "Guess, sirrah. Guess," she said as if this were a school-yard game.

The boys on the bridge watched them now. Will

could feel their eyes examining him and his sister. They'd tell their parents if he wasn't careful. "Saw Will, the glover's boy, beating his sister on the bridge." Then everyone in town would know.

Will stopped shaking Joan. "Tell me," he hissed, "or I'll break your arm."

His sister hiccuped. "Oh, aren't you fearsome?"

He scowled. This tormenting game delighted her too much. He let go of her and took a step toward town. "I'll find out on my own."

"Better not."

He turned. "Why?"

"Because you're the cause."

Suddenly his legs felt as limp and weak as the soft, rotted reeds along the riverbank. *Few secrets hid. Most desires known.*

"They found Mopsa this morning caught up along the rocks."

"Mopsa?" He leaned against the bridge railing. "Mopsa?"

"I saw them pull her out. Some said she must have slipped and fallen. There was a bucket nearby. But she was too far away from home to be going for water."

Will felt his legs go wobbly. "She willfully drowned herself?" It seemed impossible. Mopsa with the warm thighs, the deep laugh. Dirty, carefree Mopsa who'd do anything he asked. Anything.

"When they fished her from among the reeds and willows, her hair hung like soaking dark rags," Joan continued. She wasn't talking to him anymore. She was merely reciting what she'd seen. She turned away from him and spoke slowly, carefully, as if she was trying to remember every detail behind her closed eyes. "Starting to bloat like pulpy skins in the white right before the last tanning rinse. Someone had the presence of mind to cover her with a blanket where her clothes fell away. They picked her up and carried her to the alehouse. Those standing nearby were crying and wailing."

Will's cloak flapped open in the breeze. He felt no cold. He couldn't believe what his sister was saying. Mopsa gone. Impossible.

"One man had his hands under her armpits, her head lolling this way and that. Gray eyes open, skin blue-white. Wasn't the first dead body I ever saw, of course."

Will didn't want to listen. He wanted to put his hands over his ears. But he couldn't.

"The horror and hush of it." Joan paused and gripped the bridge railing. "Some of the women walking past or running down to the river raised their aprons to their faces to keep from looking, as if that might save them from suffering."

Will stared numbly into the water. There seemed nothing he could do now but hear his sister out to the end.

"Even before they got her up the riverbank, the rumors were spreading. How she looked like she was with child." Joan's voice sounded dull, matter-of-fact. She spoke with the same amount of emotion that she might have used to say a Latin lesson. "Since she took her own life and the unborn's, some say both had sacrificed the right to a Christian burial. She'll be cast into a hole at a crossway or refuse heap, where folk might tread upon her grave or throw broken pots and stones on it."

Will sucked in his breath hard and made a small, sudden wailing sound that surprised and embarrassed him. "They don't know for sure, do they?"

"About what?"

"The unborn." Will could barely say the word without feeling as if he might be sick.

Joan stared out at the water and shrugged. "Why walk into the river?" She turned and examined Will closely. Her eyes pierced him through and through. "Mother was right. It is always the women who suffer. Not men. You go on and on. You find new lovers. You don't care. We are the ones who are left ruined—our reputations destroyed, our names diminished."

"Now what is this you speak of?" Will blurted out, glad to have the chance to change the subject. "If Richard, that disreputable scoundrel, has—"

"Do you see?" she interrupted in a disgusted manner. "Richard does not know I exist. A silly, foolish girl—that's all I am to him. Naturally, you assume the worst. But there is no scandal except that which was created by you, no scoundrel except yourself. You should heed your own advice. 'There's eight years' difference between you.' Isn't that what you once warned me?"

Will clenched his fists. *She knows about Anne of Shottery.* He wanted to hit something. A stone wall. A face. Anything. He kicked a rock hard. It skittered across the bridge and landed with a splash in the river.

"Your secret's safe," Joan said. She refused to look at him. Instead, she seemed to peer for comfort at her shoes. "Now that I'm fourteen, I'll be leaving soon. Seven years' indenture knitting and sewing and cooking isn't so long, is it?"

Will didn't answer. He knew that when Joan left home to go into service, he'd have no one to make excuses for him. He'd have to bear on his own the full brunt of Father's scrutiny and Mother's disappointment. And there'd be his brothers to look after—Joan's old job. There'd be even less time for Will to do what he wanted.

Joan picked up another rock and pitched it into the water. "Have you ever stopped to consider that if we don't leave this place, we may never find refuge except under the dark river? All the whispering, the accusations. So many rules, so many traditions. The lies. The spying. It drives us all to madness sometimes, I think."

A small voice whispered in Will's ear, *"Broken pots and stones . . ."* Will pinched himself. He was awake. Yet nothing seemed real. Nothing. "Joan, you're not mad," Will said quickly. He tried to sound lighthearted, but his words were hollow. When he attempted to chuckle, the noise he made was more of a guilty squawk. "Now, now—"

"Don't treat me like a simpering child," Joan said coldly. "I'm not stupid. I can see very well the role you've played in what happened."

"Me? I played no role." Will felt his face flush. Now his sister had gone too far. "I never loved Mopsa. I never said I loved her. Why do you accuse me like this?"

"Because it is the truth. You killed her by giving her false hopes. I know how she felt."

"You're an ignorant girl. What do you know of love?"

Joan straightened her back and looked at him with fierce intensity. "Enough to know how hard and unhappy is our fate that love must be bestowed where it is so little valued."

"You don't know anything except what you've read in sonnets." *There.* Now she looked wounded. Furious, he turned away from Joan. To calm himself, he thought of Anne of Temple Grafton. *Pure Anne, virtuous Anne.* The woman he worshiped. The woman who would save him. What happened to Mopsa wasn't his fault. Anne would understand. Of course she would.

"You are more cruel and ignorant than I imagined," Joan said in a slow, measured voice. "What makes you think your actions have no consequences? It is quite obvious you do not understand women at all." With that she pulled her cloak hood over her head and marched away.

He watched her walk across the bridge toward town. He glanced at the gawking boys, who'd now moved down to the riverbank. They poked long sticks into the grass as if hunting for something. Some memento of death, some grisly souvenir. A lock of hair or a soggy stocking. Angrily Will waved his arms at them. He lurched off the bridge, leaping down onto the bank as if to beat them. The boys escaped, screaming.

Will stood in the long, dead grass and observed the river ripple and flow. She was gone. Mopsa was gone. He could still hear her earthy laughter echo in his head. He could still hear her down-at-the-heels shuffle across the alehouse floor. Her squeals of pleasure in the darkness. Her smoky, coarse hair on his face. Once upon a time she had been good enough company when he was bored or lonely. He couldn't believe she'd drowned. Perhaps that was not her body that they'd found. Perhaps Mopsa was only hiding somewhere as a kind of prank. *Like pretending to walk on water.*

Will wrapped his cloak around himself, but he still felt chilled. When he looked toward town, he saw in the distance a bony horse pulling a two-wheeled cart. Beside the horse stumbled an old man. *Soon I'll be like him.* One day his youth, his good looks, his ambition, would be gone. What had the hag told him? *"Thou shalt venture on a great journey while never straying farther than thy hearth, though one day thou wilt leave behind what thou lovest best."* He hoped what happened to Mopsa had nothing to do with this prophecy.

Slowly he climbed up the embankment, head down,

deep in thought. He ambled along the road to escape his sense of confusion. The sky turned darker gray. The wind felt moist and cool against his cheeks. He didn't want to go home yet, even though he was hungry and tired.

Instead, he kept walking south toward the mill. The people he encountered didn't speak to him. They held their hoods against their ears and bent forward into the wind. "Good morrow, sir," Will said to one of his father's customers, William Perrot.

Perrot ignored him and walked quickly past. For the first time, Will thought he might have become invisible. No one seemed to see him, and no one spoke to him. It was an eerie feeling. He sensed he might have become a ghost.

"Good morrow, sir," he called in a loud voice to Higges, the town's clock keeper. He did not reply. The cruel silence was unnerving. Did everyone suspect him of causing Mopsa's death, just as Joan had said? *This must be some kind of punishment.* For a moment, he sensed what it must be like to be Mopsa's severed spirit, tormented and forced to wander forever on the streets of town. A solitary ghost.

He walked and walked faster and faster until he found himself standing beside the rank reeds of the fishing ground. The gray-black water hissed. Mopsa had always been kind to him—kinder than he deserved. She always inquired after his health. She was generous to a fault.

He tried to remember her when she wasn't tipsy, wasn't ugly with too much drink or animated with too much slavish, subservient talk. He tried to picture her when her feet weren't dirty. He couldn't. And her maddening talk! She had driven him to distraction. Her talk of love. Her talk of marriage. He'd never agreed to any of it. No one could accuse him of not keeping his word. No one could say for certain the child was his. *There'd been so many men.* After all, she was an alehouse wench, the kind of woman his friends had jokingly called an easy glove—one that goes on and off with pleasure.

Will stared into the current. Without thinking, he plucked each finger and pulled his worn kid glove from his right hand. Even now he could hear Mopsa's voice. Always so eager to share the latest gossip. What had she been trying to tell him the last time he saw her? Something about a woman in the stocks. He closed his eyes, trying to remember.

"When winter comes, who'll feed the babe . . . ?"

Without thinking, Will dropped the glove into the shallow water. He felt too stunned to notice.

She'd been asking for help, and he had not listened. A sour taste rose from the pit of his stomach into his throat. The fallen glove floated and curled. *"Starting to bloat like pulpy skins . . ."*

In that moment, he had a vision of his own eternal damnation. A face flickered with a gaping, awful mouth that breathed fire—worse than anything he'd seen on the stage as a boy or heard about in church. Trembling, he leaned over and scooped up the soggy glove.

Maybe this was a sign, he told himself. A sign of Providence. Maybe this was his chance to make good, to change. Resolutely, he plucked off the left glove and tossed them both into the fast-moving current in the middle of the river. He watched his old self—sorry and disreputable—float down the river. From this day, he vowed, he'd take a new path. He'd stop drinking, fighting, stealing, disrespecting elders, and whoring. He'd stay away from his debauched, deceitful uncle and his friends. He'd give up his late-night visits to Anne of Shottery. He'd avoid the woman as if she were the plague.

The perfect, pious partner for him was none other than Anne of Temple Grafton. That much seemed clear. He'd become a secret, conscientious Catholic and follow every commandment—no matter how dangerous. And thus he'd woo and win the hand of Anne of Temple Grafton. Making her his bride, he knew, was the easiest, surest, and fastest way to save his soul and change his life forever.

Chapter Eighteen

During the next three weeks Will, the determined wooer, delivered to Anne of Temple Grafton all manner of secret gifts: an apple carved with their initials; a pair of ladies' gloves snatched from his father's shop; and a silk riband that he'd bought from the peddler very dear. These tokens of goodwill for marriage seemed to delight her, much to his surprise.

"There's something that would please me even more," she said softly one afternoon when the November sky had turned gray and glowering and there was a hint of snow in the air. Will felt comfortable and snug sitting beside Anne before her family's fire. Her father was busy in the barn, and her sister was nowhere to be seen.

"What is it?" he asked in a hopeful voice, and moved a little closer.

She pushed him away and frowned. "To take Holy Communion together in the Old Faith."

"Oh," said Will, downcast. Anne seemed so still, so contemplative, he wondered if her blood flowed. To please her, he'd spent hours memorizing catechism and prayers, citing Bible passages, and reciting the names of saints. After all this time she would not even give him the smallest kiss. Now she wanted him to celebrate Holy Communion in the Old Faith. This was dangerous business. He could be arrested and thrown in jail if he was caught in such a forbidden ceremony with a priest. Before they were publicly executed, captured priests were routinely starved, thumbscrewed, jabbed with needles under their fingernails, and lowered into dank, dark well shafts for days at a time in order to make them provide their Protestant torturers with names of recusants.

Was Anne worth such a terrible risk? He stole a glimpse of her face in the firelight. Her beauty seemed so dazzling, so distant, he decided to make a bold move. "Marry me and I'll do anything you say."

She looked surprised, then laughed. "You're still an apprentice. Your father will be fined if you marry. You know that. Besides, you're only eighteen and I'm barely seventeen. My father would never approve. You're too young. I'm too young."

Will studied her blush and could tell she was pondering his proposal. *Perhaps she likes the idea of my complete conversion.* This gave him stubborn hope. "Your father approves of me," he said. This was not a lie. Her father had told him he was delighted that Anne seemed to have given up the idea of becoming a nun. Marriage would make sure she'd never consider such a crazy religious notion again. "Let us steal our marriage and not risk refusal of my father or yours," whispered Will. "I'll go to Worcester for the marriage license. We'll marry in secret, and no one will know until we've already tied the knot. What could be simpler?"

Anne gave him a skeptical look. She stared at her hands and counted silently on her fingers. "What about the proclamation of the banns? Our marriage must be announced three times in church on successive Sundays or holy days. And with the coming of Advent, there'll soon be a prohibition. Canon law says from Advent Sunday until the Octave of Epiphany there can be no asking of banns. That means we can't be married for four more months."

Four months! Will knew he couldn't wait that long for marital bliss. Four months sounded like an eternity. In four months he might stray again into old bad habits he'd worked so hard these past few weeks to avoid. He'd stayed out of taverns. He hadn't been in a fight or broken the law once. And he'd resolutely avoided Anne of Shottery, in spite of her countless written entreaties. He doubted he could be pious four more months. He would go mad. "Why must we wait so long? I don't understand."

Anne sighed as if he were a very small, very troublesome child. "Today is November twenty-fifth. We're almost too late as it is."

"Too late?" said Will anxiously. "Too late for what?"

"A church wedding. I've always wanted a church wedding."

Will's shoulders slouched forward. He'd assumed that getting married was simple. Now it sounded much more complicated, much more painful.

Her eyes narrowed with determination. "I want a church wedding with a priest."

"A priest?" Will's voice squeaked. Involving a priest in a marriage scheme would be the most dangerous, illegal thing he'd ever done. He started to feel very ill.

She took his hand. She'd never taken his hand before. She'd never let him touch her. As she held his hand she stroked it as if it were a cat. He was so dazed, he couldn't speak. If she asked him to jump off a cliff at this moment, he would have done it. "Tomorrow we'll go and see Father Frith," she said. "He'll know what to do."

"Who is he?" Will asked, nearly dizzy. He was afraid to speak for fear she'd notice she was holding his hand, which seemed to buzz with some new kind of energy.

"The vicar of Grafton, John Frith."

Will breathed a sigh of relief. "A Protestant minister?"

She shook her head. "He's only pretending," she said in a low voice. "You mustn't tell anyone. Tomorrow come early, and we will go to him." She dropped his hand and stood. "Farewell."

"I love you beyond expression," he said in a dramatic voice, certain at last of his salvation.

"I know," she said, and made the sign of the cross. Sadly Will departed, confused and hopeful at the same time.

Will spent a sleepless night in anticipation. In the morning he desperately managed to convince Joan to lend him with interest the three shillings he needed for the marriage license. No one suspected anything when he left home and hurried in frantic haste to Temple Grafton. "I've given my family the least cause of suspicion," he congratulated himself. What a performance! He'd been the perfect, flattering, obedient son. He tried to imagine the surprise on Father's and

Mother's faces when he returned a married man. *And there won't be a thing they can do about it.*

He and Anne met secretly at the crumbling vicarage perched on a hill at Temple Grafton. From this spot Will could look across the windswept, drab-colored valley and spy Bredon Hill and the Cotswolds. Below, cows pastured in the open common. The cows faced the wind as they grazed what was left of yellow hay stubble.

"Good morrow, Father," said Anne to a hobbling old man who opened the door. He didn't seem surprised to see her. He simply held up a perched hawk sitting on his gloved wrist. The bird of prey leaned forward and glared at Anne and Will.

Will found the bird's fierce, mirrorlike eyes and powerful talons disconcerting. Hawks like these were used for hunting rabbits and smaller birds. Will winced when he caught a whiff of the overpowering stench inside the vicar's stone house—a mixture of feathers and dead mice and bird excrement. Will bumped his head on the low doorway as he entered. He was surrounded by wicker cages that hung from the ceiling and stood stacked on the floor. Each cage contained a hawk or falcon that shrieked with ear-piercing intensity.

"Be calm, my lovelies!" the vicar said in a loud voice. Eventually the birds quieted themselves, but only after much hopping and rattling of cages, much flapping of enormous wings. The birds stared at Will with hungry, sideways glances through the slats. He had never before been surrounded by so many birds of prey. "My chief trade," said the vicar, giving the falcon a fond rub beneath her razor-sharp beak, "is to cure hawks that are hurt or diseased, for which purpose many do usually repair to me."

Will nodded. "You are also a minister?"

"I do not consider that anything can happen without the permission of a just God," the vicar replied, and smiled.

Will looked helplessly at Anne. He wondered if this old man might be mad.

"Father," said Anne, "we wish to be married tomorrow."

"Have thou a falcon for me?" the vicar asked in a tremulous voice.

Anne shook her head. "We need your advice and your help."

"Thou seems of a discreet, sober, and religious temper," the vicar replied. "Do I know thee, child?"

"You do," she said in a patient voice. "I am Anne Whateley, Father. You've known me all my life. You baptized me. You gave me my first Holy Communion. You are my family's priest."

The vicar looked at her with his mouth half-open, so that the gaps between his teeth stared like windows. The bird rubbed its head against its breast, then ruffled its feathers all at once. "Ah, yes. Now I recall. What troubles thee, dear child?"

"Can you tell us how we can marry in secret?" she said in a low voice.

"In secret?" said the vicar. He scowled. "Take heed of what thou does, for there's nothing done in secret that will not come to light."

"We need to know about the banns and the license and how to avoid the prohibition during Advent. Can you tell us, Father?"

Will was beginning to feel as if the stink of birds and lack of air in the room might choke him. The hawks scowled at him with a greedy unhappiness. Did they wish that he, too, were caged? The vicar stroked the bird. He reached into a sack and pulled out a dead mouse. He held it by the tail and allowed the hungry falcon to tear it to pieces.

"Thou must go to Worcester to the diocesan consistory court and apply for a special marriage license that will allow only one saying of the banns—perhaps at the church door at the time of the ceremony," said the vicar. "To secure a license thou will need a sworn allegation, giving the name, address, and occupation of the parties and of the consenting parents, and the reason for dispensing with full publication."

"Can you provide this, Father?" Anne pleaded.

"I suppose," the vicar replied doubtfully. "I can neither preach nor read well anymore. If thou will write it for me, I will sign, dear child."

Anne smiled. "What else?"

"Then thou receives a license that's kept by me, to whom it's addressed. The clerk of the court records the license in the bishop's register. And then thou will be free to marry in a church ceremony. Come hither at noon tomorrow, and I will gladly perform the ceremony in the chapel. It is a poor, mostly unused place these days. Thou knows the place?"

Anne nodded with delight. "And you will give Will and me Holy Communion as well?"

"When the sun's not in my eyes, I know a hawk from a heron," the vicar said. "Who is Will?" The falcon gobbled the last of the mouse.

"I am, sir," Will said. He could not stop watching the bird, whose face feathers were sticky with blood.

The vicar placed the preening bird of prey on a wooden perch in the middle of the room. Then he removed his large leather gauntlet. He turned to Will. "Does thou have a falcon for me?"

"No, sir," said Will.

The vicar studied him carefully, as if he, too, were an injured bird. "Are thy fancies giddy and unfirm? More longing, wavering, sooner lost and won?"

"No, sir," said Will, hoping that was the correct answer.

"Remember," the vicar said in a low voice, "women are as roses, whose fair flower being once displayed doth fall that very hour."

Will nodded, even though what the vicar said strained him past the compass of his wits. The vicar's words didn't sound the least bit religious. Meanwhile, Anne had been carefully writing down the necessary information on a piece of paper. She handed the paper to the vicar, who signed his name with a trembling hand. "Take this to Worcester," he said to Will. Will took the paper and folded it carefully.

"We'll come tomorrow, Father, at noon to be wed," Anne said eagerly. She made the sign of the cross.

The vicar lifted his hand and blessed her. "Hold, daughter. I do spare a kind of hope. Believe in God and you will be safe."

Anne took Will by the hand and walked with him from the vicar's house. Together they followed the path down the hill toward the road that led toward town. She surprised Will by walking arm in arm much farther on the road than was her usual custom. "I will go to Worcester for the license first thing in the morning. Then I'll return, and we'll meet at the vicar's at noon," he said happily.

They paused at the crossroads where she'd turn back for Temple Grafton. She smiled at him and lifted her face like a flower. The sight delighted him. She was inviting him to kiss her for the first time, and he eagerly obliged.

"Pure lips, dear saint!" he exclaimed, stunned by her delicious softness. He felt so light-headed, he seemed to hover several inches from the ground. "Sweet seals imprinted! Because of you my sin is purged. Kiss me again." When he tried to embrace her once more, she pushed him away.

"Good morrow," she said, blushing. "Until our wedding day."

Will exploded into a run. Dizzy with happiness, he thought he might soar skyward on feathered wings. Neither November wind nor damp chill bothered him. He was oblivious to everything except thoughts of his own future pleasures—unaware that from across the field a hunched figure never once stopped staring at him.

Chapter Nineteen

The next morning, in the damp, cold darkness before sunrise, Will borrowed from an unsuspecting neighbor a swaybacked horse and rode twenty-one miles to Worcester. He trotted fast and hard, certain that if he did not spur the horse on, he would lose his nerve and turn back. Inside his wallet he carried the three shillings and the letter from the vicar of Grafton, John Frith, certifying that no lawful impediment existed to keep him from marrying Anne Whateley.

To his amazement the clerk with rheumy eyes did not question his age, his suitability, or his motives. Will paid his fee, and the clerk entered the license in the bishop's register:

27 November 1582
Wm Shaxpere et Anna Whateley de Temple Grafton

"Now thou art free to marry," the clerk said, and coughed into an ink-spotted rag.

Will trotted the exhausted horse back to town. He was breathless and full of expectation. What luck! There seemed to be no obstacle to his happiness. He had only to reach the vicar's church in Temple Grafton and the ceremony would be performed. At last he'd have what his heart desired most: Anne, the woman who would change his life and save him from damnation.

When he reached town again, his stomach growled. He'd eaten nothing all day. He was tired and mud-spattered from the hard ride. Was this any way for a bridegroom to look? To fortify himself, he decided to slip inside the Swan. He'd have a quick drink perhaps and a bite to eat, and then scurry home, change his clothing, and then on to Temple Grafton. *Plenty of time.* He praised himself for his cleverness. *I've accomplished so much, and it's more than an hour till the noon bell rings.* He dismounted and tied the horse to a hitching post.

A fire burned brightly in the hearth, where men gathered and roasted crab apples and dropped them hissing into their beer. The crowded room smelled of woodsmoke, damp wool, and unwashed bodies. For a moment, he thought of Mopsa. How odd not to find her here. To keep his mind off such unhappy thoughts, he glanced about the group of customers. Something hummed among the loud voices—a voice that sounded peculiarly familiar. Who was it? Will listened as he sipped from a tankard of small beer. "Who's come?" Will asked a fellow drinker.

"Players," the man grunted. "And that Alleyn fellow."

The Earl of Worcester's Men had returned!

Will pushed back from the bench and stood. He scanned the crowd. Across the semidark room he heard a piercing tenor voice that seemed to rise above the rest. And once again Will remembered: *"You should do what gives you passion."*

Anxiously he ran his hand through his hair. *Might the little man still remember me?* All of Will's hunger and fatigue vanished. Some joy long hidden returned. Will didn't know why. The feeling was akin to drinking a cold, deep draft of clean water in August's heat or standing beside a roaring fire after enduring bitterly cold wind.

This must be a sign. As if in a dream, he knew exactly what he must do. He stood, raised his tankard to the players, and in a bold voice said, "To the Earl of Worcester's Men!"

"Hear, hear!" someone shouted. Tankards thumped on the wooden tables.

Alleyn struggled to his feet and climbed atop a bench. He wobbled and peered through the semi-darkness in Will's direction. "Look, gentlemen, a local citizen who knows quality."

Alleyn's fellow actors cheered.

"Join us, sir!" the little man called.

Will wasted no time. He wove among the benches and made a small bow before taking a seat at the actors' crowded table.

"Welcome," said the little man. The chin of his large head came barely over the top of the table. He waved his tankard. "You're the fighter. I know you."

Will nodded, a bit embarrassed.

"With swords?" Alleyn demanded.

"With fists," the little man said. He scuttled up atop the bench and stood so that he could be better heard. "This young hero graciously served as my second, although I had no need of his help. I handled the ruffians very well on my own." He paused and took a long sip of sack. "You're the one with the memory."

Will shrugged sheepishly.

"Here's a fellow who can fight and say any speech," said the little man. "We could use a fellow like this one now that Sly's gone."

"Poor Sly." One of the actors held his hat over his heart.

"A tragedy—that knife between his ribs," agreed another. "What talent lost."

"Aye," his companion replied. "He was a heedless trusting fellow. He should have suspected his lover's husband might come home unannounced."

"We shall miss him," said Alleyn, who hefted his tankard aloft. "To Sly, wherever he is. May he rest in peace."

"To Sly," the others repeated solemnly in a toast. More drinks were called all around. Will's tankard was refilled.

"What other talents do you possess, sir?" Alleyn said.

As Will drank, he felt bolder. He cleared his throat, then paused. What if his neighbors heard him boast? They'd ridicule his ambitions and make his life miserable. "I write poetry," he said in a modest voice. "I know some Latin and a little Greek."

"We've not much use for poets," Alleyn said, and sniffed.

"Unless your name's John Heywood," replied the little man.

Alleyn leaned with his elbows on the table and peered at Will. "Can you sing and dance?"

"Passably well, sir," said Will.

"We are sometimes in need of a prompter," said the little man.

"Pray, what's that?" asked Will, hoping he didn't seem too ignorant.

Alleyn smiled broadly. "Someone to pick up and remind us of lines when we forget. I never forget. But these fellows sometimes do."

His companions hooted.

"We'll be hard-pressed to perform our usual repertoire without Sly," said the little man. "We need someone to work the thunder and carry the spears. Why not give this hardy fellow a chance?" Then he turned to Will. "There'd be pay, though not much. It's a chance to see the world outside this plash of pond."

Alleyn crossed his arms in front of himself. "Are you free to join us? We leave tomorrow for London."

Will forgot everything at that moment. He could not remember how to speak, how to breathe.

"Say something, man!" said Alleyn in a bright voice. "Or do you have a stutter?"

"Perhaps he has a wife and squalling brat at home waiting," joked one of the actors.

"A wife and child's an encumbrance," said another with a nod.

Will scarcely heard anything they said. The only

words ringing in his ears were: *join us* and *London*. He gulped. "Yes," he said finally. "Yes, I'll come."

"Good!" exclaimed the little man. He jumped up on the table. "Meet us here at the inn tomorrow at sunrise. We set out for London then."

One of the older players announced in a brisk voice, "Let us make haste. We have parts to prepare. Alleyn, you may have to play the wench."

Alleyn made a terrible groan. The wench was ordinarily a boy's part, the role given to the one whose voice had not yet changed. Clearly he wasn't pleased at the prospect of wearing a dress.

"All right, I come." Alleyn took one last swig of his ale and thumped the empty tankard down on the table. "One must be adaptable in this business. Are you adaptable, Poet?" He studied Will.

Will nodded. He'd do anything—wear a dress, a beard, a monkey's head—for a chance to escape. He lifted his tankard in a final toast. "Tomorrow, sir."

The noon bell rang in the cathedral. Will hastily wiped his mouth with the back of his hand and sprang from the bench. He'd completely forgotten. He was supposed to be in Temple Grafton, where Anne waited for him at the vicar's church. *She'll understand. She's an angel.* He'd have to think of some way to convince Anne of his new plan, his new occupation. He could do it, he felt certain. After all, he'd convinced her to marry him, hadn't he?

He dashed through the door. The words, the promises of the actors, filled him with such strong expectation and hope, he had only to pump his arms to float up above the tops of the trees. *And, oh, why not go higher?*

Will quickly untied the jaded horse from the hitching post. As he was about to sling his leg over the horse he felt a strong hand grapple him by the shoulder and yank him to the ground.

"Where, sirrah, do you think you're going?"

Dazed, Will stared up into the faces of two burly yeomen, Fulke Sandles and John Richardson. Everyone knew that these two well-off farmers were beholden to favors from Sir Lucy. Sandles grappled Will's cloak hood and held him choking by the neck, the way he might grab a hare by the ears. Now what awful thing had Uncle Hal said about him? *The great betrayer.*

"What do you want?" Will gagged, and tried to swing a punch. The two men dodged his fist and clamped hold of him tighter. He struggled to twist free. "Let me go!" Will cried.

"When hell freezes over," said Sandles.

Richardson frowned. "You're coming with us." He and Sandles hoisted Will under each arm and marched him in a humiliating fashion up Back Bridge Street. The old horse followed them.

"Why?" demanded Will. Panic-stricken, he thought of Anne Whateley waiting for him at the church. "I haven't broken any laws. Let me go on my way."

Sandles and Richardson shot each other meaningful looks. They seemed to take great pleasure dipping and dragging Will's feet through every available dung heap they passed. Fascinated onlookers stopped and stared. They whispered eagerly, as if they'd always known that a dawcock like Will would come to no good.

"We trespassed, yes," Will pleaded, "but I didn't harm one rabbit. Not one. And you know yourself, sir, that everybody brawls. Even your son when he has a bit of drink in him, sir, and I don't think anyone was severely injured. And as for that other prank, sir, I meant nothing by it. Just a pair of timbrels floating on the water."

Richardson snorted. He gave Will a sharp kick in his behind to make him walk faster up Henley Street. "Don't try anything more foolish than you've already done."

"Aye, don't even think about escaping out of this one," said Sandles.

Will's aching, twisted shoulders felt as if they might be wrenched loose. *They're taking me home. Good.* He'd explain everything to Father. Father would get rid of them. And then he'd find the chance he needed to slip out of sight and escape to Temple Grafton.

Sandles pounded with his beefy fist on Father's shop door. The door opened quickly, as if they were expected. Father's face looked bright red. He glanced from Sandles to Richardson, not once letting his eyes rest on his son. Father hurriedly signaled for them to bring Will inside, as if embarrassed that neighbors were watching.

Will tripped and plunged through the doorway. Sandles and Richardson stood solid as a wall before the closest exit. Desperately Will surveyed the shop. Mother had positioned herself before the bolted back entrance. Her proud, angry expression looked as implacable and hard as slate. Beside her slouched Joan, who refused to meet his gaze. His brothers cringed uncertainly near the worktable.

"So you found him," Father growled.

Richardson nodded. "He was trying to escape on a horse."

"My neighbor's," Father replied.

"I was going to bring it back," Will said. "If this is about the stolen horse, I swear I was going to—"

"Quiet!" Father barked. "This is not about a horse. It's about something much more serious. These two men are friends of the late Master Hathaway. They're bondsmen who've posted forty pounds—a goodly sum of money that's not lightly risked. They've posted their own money to make sure you do your duty."

"Duty—" Will squeaked.

"Matrimony," interrupted Sandles with some impatience. "Anne Hathaway's quick. The child brags in her belly already. She says 'tis yours. Don't pretend you don't know anything about it. We've plenty of witnesses to your trysts."

Will was too dumbfounded to speak. *This can't be true.* His father's furious face wavered before him. All Will could think about was how he must escape, how he must find some way to get out of the shop and hurry to Temple Grafton. Anne was waiting for him. Anne, the woman he wanted to marry. *This is all some horrible mistake.*

Chapter Twenty

For several moments no one spoke. The only sound in the room was the whimpering of Edmond as he sucked his thumb.

"Will, pay attention," Father said sharply. "Because of the lateness of the day, you're going to Worcester with Hathaway's neighbors for a special license. You'll stay the night at Worcester, get the license tomorrow in the morning, then return for the church service at Luddington. An out-of-the-way church. No neighbors to gawk about." Father coughed nervously.

More scandal. More disgrace. Will sensed Father's obvious discomfort. There'd be plenty of gossip about an eighteen-year-old boy marrying a woman nearly eight years his senior.

"Then," Father continued, "you'll both come here to live."

Will started. *Anne of Shottery living here?* He could hardly imagine anything more improbable. She'd never even officially met his parents. And now he was supposed to marry her and come to live in this house that was already crowded with his three noisy brothers and his sister?

"Will, are you hearing anything I'm saying?" Father demanded.

Will nodded dully.

Joan began to weep. She made no effort to restrain herself or conceal her tears. Her piercing keening seemed to suck the remaining air, light, and hope from the room.

"Hush, girl!" Father said.

Joan sniffled. Will squirmed. *This can't be happening.* He was about to be married for life, with no hope of escape.

Sandles pinched his shoulder hard. "According to Hathaway's will, Anne's to receive six pounds thirteen shillings and four pence on the day of her marriage. This will be used for the dowry."

Will blinked, the pain in his shoulder was so fierce. He didn't care about a dowry. *My arm!* He couldn't cry out. He closed his eyes to keep from having to see his sister's pale, wet face or the terrified expressions of his ghostlike brothers.

"Even though you are a minor, Will," Father continued, "I cannot go with these gentlemen to Worcester with you, because if I do, I will be charged a steep fee for allowing my apprentice to marry." His cheeks mottled a deeper red, as if the very act of saying these words filled him with pain. "You can never know how disappointed we are by what you've done."

Will took a deep breath. "I am sorry, sir," he mumbled. He was supposed to be marrying Anne of Temple Grafton. He was supposed to be joining the theater company tomorrow at sunrise. He had a whole new life mapped out for himself, and now none of it was going to happen. His life was over.

"Come along!" said Sandles, who swung open the door and gave Will a sharp prod in the back.

"May I have a moment with my son, sir?" Father asked.

Richardson yanked then steered Will in his father's direction. In spite of the shop's crowded conditions, Father acted as if he and Will were speaking in private. "There's nothing I can do to save you," Father whispered. "You've only yourself to blame for what's happened. Nobody else. Be a man and face this. You understand?"

"Yes, sir." Will glanced at his father with the desperation of drowning Icarus. Richardson grabbed

Will's arm again and pushed him outside the door into the street, where three fresh horses were waiting. The wind howled along Henley Street. Icy rain soaked Will's clothing.

"Don't try anything foolish," Sandles said to Will as the three of them mounted their horses.

"You attempt to escape," added Richardson, "we'll hunt you down. Then we'll kill you."

Will rode single file between Sandles and Richardson to Worcester for the second time that day. It was the longest, most uncomfortable journey of his life.

A procession marched to the church, where vows were said outside the door. Hastily the Luddington vicar gave a blessing indoors before a crowd of faceless onlookers. Drink was shared as a sign of friendship between the families, followed by a meal at the Hathaway home in Shottery.

Afterward, Will remembered nothing of the details of these events. For him the past twenty-four hours sloughed away like the last dead leaves fallen from trees. He had no memory of any word, any action, any sound except his sister's sniffling that echoed through the drafty church.

The wedding, Will decided, was more like a

funeral. His funeral. Father and Mother did their best to keep up appearances. Father presented fine wedding gloves to Anne's haughty stepmother. Mother brought a spice custard pie she'd made while Will was hustled off to Worcester. But there was no joy, no hope in the wedding feast, because there was no joy, no hope in the bride or bridegroom.

Hours later Will slouched fully clothed against the wall upstairs in the drafty chamber over the shop, the place that was to be the bride and bridegroom's chamber. He sprawled on the floor, knees up, feeling numb from too much to drink. Stupidly he squinted at his muddy hose and shoes covered with grime from that day's eighty-two miles on the road—farther than he'd ever traveled in his life. *And as far as I'll ever go.*

Wind rattled the chamber shutters and blew through chinks in the walls' wattle. At great expense Father had given them a candle, which stood in a pewter stand—a gift from Anne's sister.

Anne perched on the opposite side of the room atop the bed in a feather counterpane she'd brought from home. She wore her nightdress, and her hair hung in two long braids about her shoulders. Even in this faint light her face looked tired, wan. Her shadow wavered against the wall. Her pale fingers quickly unbraided her auburn tresses. Will had never seen her hair undone in decent light. She looked different than he'd imagined. She looked older.

"Who was she?" Anne asked in an even voice.

"Who?" Will replied in surprise.

"You know who I mean. The woman that my shepherd saw you with on the road from Temple Grafton."

"No one." Will sighed. So it had been old Whittington who told his mistress. The shepherd had spied on him and started all these misfortunes.

"She must have a name."

Will took a deep breath. "Anne. Her name's Anne." Will felt worse thinking about Anne of Temple Grafton again, recalling all the suffering he must have caused her. How long had she waited at the vicar's church? *She must hate me.*

"You haven't asked about when the baby'll be born."

Will studied his bent knees. He hadn't even thought about the baby. The idea was horrifying and unreal at the same time. He knew nothing of babies except what he recalled about his disgusting brothers as toddlers. The idea that there would be a baby seemed impossible. Anne didn't even look pregnant, as far as he could tell. "Well, yes, I have considered it," he lied. He tried to ignore the sudden queasy feeling in his stomach. "Does it . . . does it have a time you know to be born?"

"Spring," Anne said, and stared at the ceiling. She looked unhappy that he wasn't more interested. He couldn't help himself. The idea of being a father was preposterous. Outlandish. "What's that noise?" She pulled the coverlet up to her chin. From outside the shuttered window on the street below, pans clanged and spoons beat against pots.

"The neighbors," said Will. He slouched forward even more. "A bit of rough music, I suspect. For our wedding day."

"Rough music?" said Anne. "To make fun of us? I'll have none of this." Eyes flashing, she whipped off the coverlet and trotted barefoot across the wooden floor to the window.

"Don't," Will pleaded.

She turned and glared at his cowardice. She shoved open the shutters and leaned out the window, so that her dark hair flew in all directions. "Who goes there?" she shouted.

"Parishioners!" someone yelled, and beat a pot with great gusto.

"Go away!" Anne bellowed.

The pots banged louder.

"Why," Anne demanded, "do you torment us?"

"You being of some years and Will being but a boy!" someone hooted.

Will wished he could crawl under the bed and never come out again.

Pots clanged. "You did so foolishly match with someone so young as him!" a neighbor called.

"Such a boy for a husband!"

"Come away from the window," Will said, mortified. "It will do no good to shout at them. You can be heard up and down Henley Street." Suddenly he saw his whole life pass in front of his eyes. His brazen, too-loud wife shouting out of windows, cursing passersby. He'd be trapped with this woman of the enormous voice for eternity. A kind of hell, a punishment for all his past transgressions.

"My back is broad enough," Anne called down, "to bear all your mocks and flouts. But though Will be a boy, he may be a man one day by grace of God, and I will not forsake him while there is breath in my body." She slammed the shutters shut and stomped across the room and jumped into bed. She pulled the blanket up over her neck again and lay hidden deep in the pillow so that Will could not see her face.

Will was stunned. *While there is breath in my body.* The pot banging ceased. The silence sounded deafening. Quietly he tiptoed across the room and blew out the candle.

"Are you coming to bed?" she asked in a muffled, hopeful voice.

"Later," he said, and slipped out the door and down the steps to the shop. In the darkness the haphazard piles of hides appeared as black chaos come again. The putrid, familiar smell of tanning choked him. Anxiously he peered out the shutter to make sure the mob had disappeared. Wrapping his cloak about himself, he stole outside to the street.

Chapter Twenty-One

A cat, tail up, prowled along the gutter as if it had nowhere to go. *Neither do I.* Will wandered down Henley Street, bent forward in a bitter wind. He clutched his cloak tight about himself. The night felt as dark and hopeless as his heart. Everyone was asleep, rushes snuffed. Will trudged on through the foul night. He considered going for a drink at the Swan, but even this was shuttered.

He walked down Back Bridge Street, a way so familiar, even in the dark he knew where to step. East, toward the river, toward the road to Shipston and then on to London. By now Alleyn and the others were probably on their way to the glorious city where anything was possible. Although Will longed to follow them, he hesitated atop the arched back of Clopton Bridge.

From below the bridge lingered the dank smell of rotting sedges. Ice narrow as a knife's blade crusted the edge of weedy shallows. Beyond the shallows the water tumbled, slabbered, and spilled over fallen logs and bigger rocks. The voice of this stretch of river seemed much louder by night than it did by day.

Will paused and listened to the foaming and raging, so much fiercer for being obstructed. The chaos of that watery voice echoed the chaos inside his mind. The rage of being trapped here—staying where he did not wish to be, encumbered with a woman he did not love, awaiting the birth of a child he could not imagine.

Someone had once told him, "Wedlock forced is hell." Now he understood. As hard as he could, he hurled a rock toward the loudest part of the river. Somewhere a water rat might be slithering among the riprap. He pitched another rock, harder this time. He tried to imagine clobbering the rat with a rock—crushing its skull. At first there was some satisfaction in that violent act. He threw another, then another. *Thunk! Thunk!*

Soon he grew tired of the pointlessness of trying to kill rats he couldn't see. He shuffled off the bridge to the other side of the river. Beneath the arch the current hissed. The river traveled far away from this town, this plash of pond. The sound mocked him. He wiped his hands on his cloak. He should keep moving. It was 120 miles to London. If he walked without stopping, he would be there in four days.

He had no food, no money. The wind blew harder, colder. He peered into the darkness of the road toward Shipston and recalled the day he went to Temple Grafton and came upon the beggar. How long would it be before Will was pelted with rocks to keep him from lingering too long in a town where no one knew him? How long before he nearly starved if not for the generosity of strangers?

Will scuffed the toe of his shoe in the gravel and tried to imagine what he would do if he made it to London. Such a big city—he'd simply disappear. He'd change his name. No one—not even beefy Sandles or Richardson—would be able to find him. What then? Where would he live? What would he do? He could try to track down the place where the Earl of Worcester's Men were lodged. But what if they had already hired someone for the job they'd promised him? He could try to find Richard and beg him to come to his aid, but why should he? Richard probably still hated him.

"*To-whit-too-who!*" an owl called.

Will shivered. *The voice of death.* How long before anyone noticed he was gone? And then what would become of Anne and his unborn child? He cringed thinking of the rough music, the taunts of neighbors, the anger of his parents. *"How disappointed we are by what you've done."* The sad surrender in his father's eyes. Another Great Misfortune.

Discouraged, Will turned, left the road, and descended the riverbank. His life had become pointless—all hope gone.

Below the bridge stood a deep pool where nothing obstructed the current and the river flowed smoothly with a gentle murmur. How easy to enter here and slip like butter down the river's throat. He took another step and felt the squelch of water coming up through the mud, through the soles of his shoes.

The frigid water bit his skin and surprised him—like sudden knowledge. Now he knew. This was how Mopsa had felt when she waded to her ankles, then to knees, thighs, waist into the swirling water beneath the willows. He imagined how she shut her eyes and sank. How her hair floated and tangled. Her coarse hair. How did it look—like seaweed, like the leaves of lilies, like stems of coronet weeds there on the water?

Will paused. Not until this moment did he understand her despair, her utter hopelessness. *Abandoned and with child.* He felt truly ashamed of himself, of his lies. If he'd told Mopsa the truth, would that have kept her from such a muddy death? "I never loved you," he murmured to the dark water. "I never intended to marry you."

No one answered. No one forgave him.

He couldn't wiggle his toes. His soggy feet had lost all feeling. What if he were to walk down into the river's depths? He told himself that his body would only suffer temporary pain. Then complete numbness would take over. A kind of watery sleep—dreamless, painless.

"'A rough, unordered mass of things,'" he proclaimed from Ovid in a loud voice, and stepped deeper. Ice shattered beneath the soles of his shoes, sharp sounding as glass. Another step. Crunch. "'The gods have their own rules.'" The water licked up around his calves. Another step. "'I see and approve better things, but follow worse.'"

This seemed so easy. Much easier than he'd imagined. There was nothing anyone could do to stop him. Nothing. He closed his eyes and leaned forward with his arms outstretched. Is this what Icarus felt when he plunged into the cold, deep blue that hushed his cries?

Splash!

Icy water stung his face, his neck. His soaked clothes turned heavy as ballast and tugged him lower, lower. The sensation of falling woke him. He struggled to stand. He flailed his arms to regain his balance. He could not. Every motion of resistance only seemed to make his escape more impossible. The bottomless slime of the riverbed sucked under his feet, his legs.

He pitched backward. His cloak tangled his arms. In the black night of black water, every direction seemed confused—up, down, river, shore. *"Be a man . . ."* His father's voice. He splashed and choked and thrashed. This was wrong. This was all wrong. This wasn't what he wanted. He wanted to live.

A light bobbed from above, on the bridge. "Who goes there?"

"Ignore that." The chuckling of some demon in his ears. *"Try, try again."*

He gulped more water. Numbness gnawed at his chin, his cheeks. It penetrated his ears. He flopped forward. His arms heavy, useless. *"Don't go too low, or the water will weight your wings down."* Soon he'd be transformed into pebble, fish bone, shell . . . down . . . down . . . down.

Suddenly something caught him by the back of the neck and hauled him to shore. A tugging, an awful tugging. His cloak was wrenched off. He wobbled and slipped and tangled in water and slime, but the hands were very strong. "Come on, man!" the hoarse voice shouted. "You mad?"

Will vomited up the river. He bent, and water spewed from his mouth. He clenched and unclenched his fists. Yet he felt nothing. Was he dead? A bright light shone in his eyes.

The night watchman held aloft a torch. "Your lips is blue," he said. "Come on, now. Take a swig."

Will looked up from his hands and knees at his rescuer. Did the man have wings? From beneath some great dark folds that hung from his neck, the watchman produced a leather bottle. He uncorked it and held it to Will's trembling mouth.

Will couldn't feel the liquor spill down his neck inside his doublet. He was too frozen to swallow. The watchman extinguished the torch. He flung one of Will's arms over his shoulder, grabbed him by the waist, and hauled him up the embankment. "You seem sober enough. Only a drunk would try and swim in this weather. Come along, now, sir. Up you go. That's good. Keep walking. Henley Street, isn't it?"

"Nn-nn-nn," said Will. His teeth chattered uncontrollably. He could not form words. His shoes made a sucking sound with every step. Somehow the sound made him want to laugh. But he couldn't. His dancing teeth wouldn't let him.

"You is lucky I was going past. Heard someone

speaking down there. Not an ordinary place to hear verse this time of night."

"Nn-nn-nn," said Will. He wanted to explain, but his tongue was attached to the roof of his mouth.

"Ovid is it?" said the watchman. "Well, I heard it before. My son, you might remember him, was in your class at school. Name's Robert. Died of the sweats last year. God bless him. Poor boy. He practiced and practiced for those orations schoolmaster made you give before everyone, but he could never remember. I helped him best I could, even though I can't read so well, but it made no difference. He forgot everything the day he had to get up in front of everyone. You never did, did you, sir? You always remembered. You was always a gentlemanly speaker, Will."

"Nn-nn-nn," Will murmured. He remembered Robert, the watchman's son, lurking in the back of the classroom, the black moons of his fingernails, his hair hanging in lanky, dark strands over his dull eyes. "Ss-ss-ss-sorry," Will struggled and spit to form a word to express his condolences. He'd forgotten all about Robert until this moment. Robert who was his age. Robert who died of the sweats.

"Can't tell you how much I miss him. Being a father is a painful experience, aye, sir. If I could, I'd have all young men sleep from when they's ten till when they's twenty-and-three. Then I'd have them wake up, grown. All that whoring, and fighting, and drinking, and disrespecting elders. It's a lamentable age. And yet my son, if I could bring him back, I would. Wild as he was. He was my son and I loved him dear." The night watchman's strides were longer than Will's, and he walked with a kind of painful speed that sent shocks up Will's legs. "Feel anything?"

Will tried to nod.

"Good, good. Now keep walking, man. We're nearly there."

Will's teeth chattered more wildly. His jaw felt as if it might come unhinged. They rounded the corner.

"Not far to go. That's a good boy." He halted and shifted Will's arm from his neck so that he could pound on the door with his fist.

In an instant, there was Father peering out with a flickering taper. His hair stood up in white tufts as he knuckled the sleep from his eyes. "Will?" he said.

"Father. Ss-ss-ss-sorry." Will tumbled into the doorway. "Sorry."

"You're wet," Father said, stunned. "What happened?"

Will tried to form words. "Been ss-ss-swimming."

Father shot a glance at the night watchman.

"He's all right, John," said the night watchman. "An accident near the bridge—nothing more. Could happen to anyone. I'll be going. Congratulations."

"For what?" asked Father.

"The new bride and bridegroom."

Father nodded and thanked him. He closed the door. Will collapsed on a bench. He sat hunched forward, gripping his elbows and shaking. Something slipped around his shoulders. Something dry, warm. There was a hot drink in his hands. He didn't know where it came from.

"Take a sip, slow now," said a woman's voice.

He looked up. It was Anne in her nightgown. She tilted her head to one side as if studying him intently, memorizing his face.

"Get you to your bed, Will," said Father, his voice stern. "You're a married man now."

Will nodded. He held the cup to his bottom lip until it felt as if it might blister. The painful sensation brought him fully back to life. And then he remembered the night watchman's words. *"He was my son and I loved him dear."* "Father?" Will had trouble forming the word.

"What now?"

"Do you hate me?"

"Fie!" Father said gently. He coughed, brushed something from his eye with his sleeve. "It's been a busy day. Go put on some dry clothes before you catch your death of cold."

Chapter Twenty-Two

Winter sunk its teeth. In the snow-covered pasture the cows' breath billowed like clouds. Iron-hard garden earth was searched for any remaining roots. Threshers in the barn labored from first light to last, using flails to separate grain from chaff. Grain was hauled along icy roads to the mill for grinding. The woodlot rang with the sound of axes cutting firewood. The blackbird left not a berry on the thorn.

There was little comfort this morning, the coldest day of the year. Joan packed her few belongings—a comb, an extra smock, a pair of stockings—inside the folds of a blanket and tied the ends tight. She was leaving the crowded, cantankerous household from which escape must have seemed welcome. Ahead lay a twelve-mile trip with Father by sledge from Henley Street to a place called Rowthorn, near Kenilworth. Joan was to work as a servant for a yeoman's family.

She was fourteen now—old enough, Mother said, to make her way in the world.

"Can you hold him, Daughter-in-law?" Mother tried to pull howling Edmond from Joan's skirt. He refused to be consoled, because he was convinced his beloved sister would never return.

Anne sighed wearily. "Come, Edmond." She grimaced when the little boy screamed louder.

"I'll take him," said Will. He didn't wish for his mother and wife to have yet another one of their quarrels on this, his sister's going-away day. "Come here, rascal." He hoisted sticky, kicking Edmond under his arm as if he were a bundle of dirty skins, then he handed the boy over to reluctant Gilbert.

"We'll see you in the summer, God willing," said Mother. She kissed Joan on both cheeks and made the sign of the cross.

"God speed you and protect you," said Anne. She lumbered across the room, rocking from side to side like a badly packed oxcart on a bumpy road. She gave Joan a stiff embrace.

The door swung open. "Father begs you to come now, Joan," her brother Richard said. He stomped his boots to shake away the snow.

Outside, Father leaned gloomily against the horse-drawn sledge. He beat his gloved hands together. A thick scarf concealed his expression.

"I'm coming, anon," Joan said impatiently. "Good-bye, good-bye." She kissed sniveling Edmond and gave a quick peck on the cheek to Gilbert and Richard.

"Farewell, Joan," said Will. He knew he'd miss her warm, clinkered spirit, her honesty. Up until this moment he never really believed such a thing might happen. His sister was leaving. With Joan gone, there'd be more work for him. And there'd be no one in the house for him to talk with about poetry or books. He'd have no one to tease and joke with, no one with whom he could banter in puns and word games.

"I've something for you, Will," said Joan with a hint of mischief. "A present. It's in the shop."

"You mustn't keep your father waiting," warned Mother.

"It will only take a moment," Joan replied, and tugged Will's sleeve. He hurried coatless behind her through the cross-passage to the shop. A small, smoldering fire in the open hearth kept the room warm.

"Look at the back of the bottom shelf where the gloves are stored." She pointed—fingernails trimmed close now, like a proper maid.

Will did as she said and found two uncut quill pens, an unfrozen bottle of ink inside a wool sack, and a dozen odd-sized sheets of paper, which Joan must have painstakingly collected from the ends of Father's receipts during the past several months.

Hungrily Will fingered the blank paper. He was speechless. "You should take this with you," he said finally.

Joan shook her head. "I've no use for writing anymore." Her voice sounded flat.

"Joan, come anon!" Mother called from the house.

Will picked up the quill and turned it over and over in his hands. It had been months since he'd written anything. The pen felt feeble and awkward between his fingers. "I'm sorry I have no keepsake for you to take, Joan."

"Do not concern yourself with such trifles. I know you've had much on your mind."

He was glad she didn't mention Anne and his troubles and disappointments. He was glad she didn't say anything about how he'd become only a shadow of his former self. He stayed out of taverns now. He didn't brawl or get arrested. Not once had he seen Uncle Hal or any of his old, wayward friends. He simply worked and ate and slept. Every day was like the next.

Joan crossed her arms in front of herself. "You have a talent," she said, "as a maker of verses." Her words surprised him almost as much as her generous gift.

"You have a talent, too," he said with all sincerity. He'd never told her this before. " 'The pallid pursuit of the world's beauty on paper.' Isn't that what you said a maker of verse does?"

Joan blushed. "Perhaps," she said slowly. "The difference is that your pursuit can save you. Mine can't."

"Joan! Daughter, come! Your father awaits you!" Mother called.

Joan looked up at Will with urgency. "Your life's become a rut-locked cart. You're going to have to get out and push. You know how, Will. Save yourself." Quickly she brushed his cheek with a kiss. "I must go. Good-bye."

"God bless and keep you," Will said. He felt something catch in his throat. His eyes burned. He blinked. Outside, he could hear the last farewells. The jingle of sleigh bells. *"Save yourself."*

He shoved away a stack of skins from the work-table and carefully trimmed the tip of one quill with a knife from his pocket. Then he picked up the bottle of ink, uncorked it, and dipped the quill inside the bottle.

What once had seemed so automatic, now required all his effort, all his concentration.

He took a deep breath and smoothed a piece of paper. He wrote:

I think I never felt so great a pain in
my life before. I could have almost been
willing to die, my anxiety and trouble were
so great. But I find myself something better
now that I have written this. . . .

He paused, uncertain where these words came from, where they were going, or what they meant. He only knew that for the first time in many months, a weight seemed to be lifting from his shoulders.

Carefully he recorked the ink bottle and replaced the pen, paper, and ink in their hiding place on the bottom shelf. He folded the paper with the writing into a small square as if it were a talisman. He needed a safe hiding place. Quickly he climbed upstairs to the chamber above the shop and slipped the folded message into the wall, inside a space between a piece of timber and some broken lathe.

Weeks passed. Snow melted. The northern wind dried up the southern dirt. The sun climbed higher in the sky again. The air was sharp but sweet when the sun shone. Grass began to peep. Tree buds opened. Frogs called. The thrush and blackbird sang a charm song among the bright red osiers.

One afternoon late in April, Anne called up to Will from the shop, "Husband, I need your help. Your father's gone to Attwood's as usual."

Will, deep in concentration in the shop chamber, didn't hear. He'd grown accustomed to shutting out the complaints of his wife as soon as they began. He spent every waking hour he wasn't working, upstairs, writing at a small table and stool he'd placed before the window. This was the one place he could escape from the cares of the tanning pit, the shop, and his quarrelsome wife, who was so large now she could not even climb the narrow stairway passage. She used a bed in the hall of the house, where she spent much of her time.

Meanwhile, Will wrote with great fury about what mattered to him and no one else. He wrote as if he were drowning and each stroke of the pen was a gulp of air. He wrote as if he were running from a fire and each page was a leap over flames that licked about his ankles and singed his hair. Like one who stood upon a promontory and spied a far-off shore, he wrote of lands he'd never visited—exotic places like Italy and Greece and unnamed tropical islands.

These were distant places, distant times he'd invented or read about in Holinshed's *Chronicles,* Montaigne's *Essays,* North's *Plutarch's Lives,* and, of course, his beloved Ovid's *Metamorphoses.*

He did not show his work to anyone. There was no one to show now that Joan was gone. Every night he collected the poems and pieces of his dreams and wanderings of his mind, and kept them safe beneath the bed.

"Worthless Husband!" Anne called more shrilly now. "Come down and bring in firewood. It is too heavy for me to lift."

Reluctantly Will put aside his pen and clambered down the stairs. He was met by frowning Anne, who stood with her hands where her hips had once been. "Pray you," she said, pointing, "undo this apron button for me. I cannot reach."

He did as he was told, then gave her back a distracted, affectionate rub. "Now is that better?"

When she turned to face him, he was surprised to see that her expression looked even more sorrowful. "You are never here to help when I need you," she complained. "I keep with you at meals, comfort you, and talk to you sometimes. Dwell I but in the suburbs of your good pleasure?"

Will shook his head. "I do not understand."

"What do you do upstairs?"

"Nothing."

"You are always so far away."

"Am I?" He opened the door that led to the garden and walked slowly to the woodpile. From somewhere in a budding elm he heard the restless song of a nightingale. One by one he picked up sticks of kindling for the hearth. *"You are always so far away."* She was right. His words had become his only escape. Maybe that was what the hag in the woods had meant when she told him he would journey far from home but never leave his hearth. Quickly he bent and picked up another piece of wood. And yet she also told him the contradiction that one day he would leave behind what he loved best. This made no sense.

As he was about to return with the armload of wood, he spied through a gap in the garden wall a young woman with flowers in her hair. She raced past laughing, followed by a young man in hot pursuit. Will watched the young man catch her round the waist and kiss her. *How long ago was I such a knave?* Will sighed. *The expense of spirit in a waste of shame.* A good line. He must write it down before he forgot.

"Come along!" cried Anne.

He glanced at the great-bellied stranger in the doorway. *This is my wife?* He shook his head and trudged toward the house again.

May arrived with a sweetness of the air that refreshed every spirit. The physician prescribed cold whey, and the apothecary gathered dew for a medicine to cure spring fever. Horses were bedecked with garlands, bells, and colored ribbons, and paraded through town. A tall young oak was cut down for the maypole. White-clad dancers frolicked beneath, in spite of Bishop Whitgift's disapproval. Fair weather made everyone reckless and merry. This month nature was full of mirth. Delight filled the senses. And why not? From the heavens came a grace and to earth, a gladness.

In the warmth and sunshine of the twenty-sixth of May, Trinity Sunday, Susanna was christened with a proper Protestant name by Vicar Henry Heicroft in the largest church in town. She was only three days old, swaddled carefully in linen bands and draped in the official embroidered bearing cloth. Almost everyone in town attended the ceremony, except Anne, who was still home abed as custom demanded.

"I baptize thee in the name of the Father, Son, and Holy Ghost. Amen," said the vicar. He dipped Susanna into the font. She wailed lustily.

"Strong lungs," whispered her proud grandfather.

Will didn't hear his father's words or notice his mother's mumbled prayer. He felt too nervous. Hands trembling, he worried he might drop the fretting infant after she was handed back to him by the official godmother, one of Anne's sisters.

As Will walked up the aisle with Susanna in his arms he sensed the eyes of everyone they passed. Most smiled and nodded. Others made secret, quick signs of the cross. "May she thrive and grow strong," said Widow Bromley.

"She's as pretty and as knowing a child as I have ever seen," said Mistress Price.

Will walked out the church door into the bright sunlight. The baby squinted. Her bright red face grew redder as she began to wail again. Awkwardly Will tried to console her by holding her against his shoulder. Parishioners filed past to express their congratulations. To Will's surprise, Susanna stopped crying. When he glanced at her again, her face had closed up like the petals of a rosebud. Her impossibly small mouth seemed no bigger than a wink.

"Good work," said Richard.

Will smiled with delight. "You came!"

"Of course. How could I stay away after I received your invitation?"

"You'll join us for some christening cheer?"

"I would be honored."

Surrounded by townsfolk and family, Richard and Will, with the baby in his arms, strolled up Church Street to Henley Street. Susanna opened her eyes a small slit as if to observe the boisterous man walking beside her father.

"And how goes business in London?" Will asked, and then felt foolish. What he wanted to say was the apology to Richard he'd rehearsed countless times.

"Business is good. Very good," Richard replied. "Fatherhood seems to suit you. One day I may follow your example, if I can ever find a proper wife." He cleared his throat. "A nunnery in France. Who would have guessed?"

Will winced. He, too, had heard the news about Anne Whateley's new vocation. "I would like to say—"

"Do not worry," Richard interrupted. "You are forgiven." He cocked his head to one side. "Look at you, a married man and a father! I can scarcely believe how you've changed. You're such a sober, proper fellow now. 'Men are April when they woo, December when they wed.' Isn't that how the saying goes? You love her very much, don't you?"

Will held the swaddled bundle tighter as they

paused before the doorway of his family's noisy house. Talkative revelers inside were busily consuming gingerbread, mince pies, fresh strawberries and cream, and kegs and kegs of ale. "I do," Will said softly. Until this moment he'd never realized how something so small, so fragile as Susanna might command such a large, strong feeling—even though he knew that at any unpredictable moment she might be snatched from him by God—like so many other infants. "She is a precious wonder."

"Your wife is fortunate her husband thinks of her with such high regard," Richard said, and winked.

Will gave his friend a halfhearted grin. He kept silent. What good would it do to correct Richard's mistaken notion? The truth, Will thought, is that maids are May when they are maids, but the sky changes when they are wives.

"Let me take her," said Will's mother, who pried Susanna from his hands. Expertly she carried the baby upstairs.

By now the celebration had spilled out of the house into the garden and the first floor of the shop. Will and Richard shouldered their way inside the house and lifted tankards in a toast. "To Susanna," said Richard, taking a sip.

"To our friendship," said Will.

"I've come to ask a favor," Richard said. "About your poetry."

Will rubbed the back of his head. "Oh, no, sir. This is how our friendship was nearly ruined once before, do you remember?"

Richard grinned. "This time I want to see if my master in London may be interested in your work. He publishes verse, you know. And it would improve my standing with him if he considers you a great find. Have you any verses to spare?"

"Of course!" said Will eagerly. He bounded around guests, hurried through the cross-passage to the shop, and rushed up the stairs. He tiptoed inside the chamber to pry away as quietly as possible the packet of hidden writing beneath the bed. He tried not to wake Anne and the baby, who were sleeping.

"What are you doing?" demanded Anne. Her face looked gaunt. She had dark circles under her eyes.

"Looking for something for a friend," he replied, and jammed the packet of papers under his arm.

"Is she not lovely?" said Anne softly. She stroked the peaceful baby's cheek with one finger. "I prayed for the right form and shape. I asked God, 'Oh, let not the sins of the parents cause Thy wrath and displeasure against the little one.'"

Will paused. The open window ushered in the soft, fragrant chant of spring wind. He studied sleeping Susanna's small, perfect mouth. "She is lovely," he said, filled with a kind of quiet awe. The baby's mouth closed and opened as if she were forming words in her sleep. What was she saying? What did she know?

He felt as if he were watching himself from a distance—as if he were in the elm looking down again on a scene on the guildhall stage. There he was beside the bed with his newborn baby and scowling wife. He smiled at the baby, such a marvel. She was the most perfect thing he had ever loved.

And suddenly he knew what happened next in the play.

One day I will leave her behind.

The skin on his neck prickled. He recalled the long-ago words of the witch in the woods. *"What thou lovest best."* This vision, this knowledge filled him with an aching sadness. The first two acts had only been a prelude for being uprooted and spirited away. And of course, this time he must go.

He wondered if Susanna would ever forgive him.

"Bring me some claret, will you, Husband?" Anne said.

The sound of her insistent voice startled Will. With care he tucked the papers under his other arm and took a step toward the stairway. Someone below strummed a lute. The shop shook with dancing, stomping, clapping, and the booming sound of Richard's voice and Father's laughter.

"No one pays any attention to the mother," Anne said, and sighed. "Ah, do not tear away thyself from me."

"I'll send something up for you to drink," Will promised.

Anne turned her closed and somber face away from him.

"I must go," he said, and gave one backward, tender glance at Susanna. Then he ducked his head slightly and headed down the narrow stairway into the bright voices, banter, and good cheer.

Author's Note

Much mystery surrounds William Shakespeare's early life. This book is based on the few surviving—often conflicting—records about his marriage at age eighteen to pregnant Anne Hathaway. On November 28, 1582, Worcester church documents show Shakespeare and Anne Hathaway of Shottery applying for a marriage license. The day before, on November 27, 1582, the clerk of the court entered the grant of a license for Shakespeare and a mysterious Anne Whateley of Temple Grafton. Who was she? No one is certain.

In 1587, when Shakespeare was about twenty-three years old, he left Stratford-upon-Avon. He went to London, where he began his career in the theater. Remaining behind in Stratford were his wife, four-year-old Susanna, and two-year-old twins,

Hamnet and Judith. Records do not show which theater company he joined first.

The London theater scene was vibrant in 1587 with the premieres of such path-breaking plays as Thomas Kyd's *The Spanish Tragedy* and Christopher Marlowe's *Tamburlaine the Great.* Early playwright John Heywood (1497–1580) had created short comedies with earthy humor that influenced Shakespeare and his contemporary English dramatists. Edward Alleyn (1566–1626) was a star in several London theater companies and in 1592 acted in Shakespeare's *Henry VI.*

Shakespeare's reputation as a talented dramatist was established by 1592—with the production of the first of the three history cycles of *Henry VI.* His first published work, the poem *Venus and Adonis,* was printed in 1593 by Richard Field's establishment and became a best-seller. In 1597 Shakespeare returned briefly to Stratford, now a wealthy man, and bought the biggest house in town.

In the course of his brilliant, twenty-four-year career, he wrote thirty-nine plays, which were performed on the London stage. He died at age fifty-two, April 23, 1616. He is considered the greatest English poet and dramatist who ever lived.

Notes on the Characters

As a work of historical fiction *The Two Loves of Will Shakespeare* makes use of facts about Stratford-upon-Avon residents in 1582 found in borough records, parish registers, wills, rent rolls, surveys, maps, and other manuscripts. This evidence offers tantalizing but brief glimpses about the friends, neighbors, and family members who were part of young Will Shakespeare's world. Like all novelists I used my imagination to create fully developed characters for this book. In doing so I was inspired by several fictional individuals Shakespeare later wrote about in his plays.

The reader may recognize in Uncle Hal some of the same boastful, hard-drinking foibles of Sir John Falstaff from *Henry IV.* Sir Worcester's Men, an actual theatrical troupe, found further elaboration in Shakespeare's rowdy players from *A Midsummer Night's Dream* and *Hamlet.* The novel's Charlecote witch owes her genesis to the famous "weird sisters" of *Macbeth*. Likewise the vicar of Grafton in *The Two Loves of Will Shakespeare* is modeled after a historical personage, John Frith, combined with a fictional creation, Friar Lawrence in *Romeo and Juliet*. Pious, protected Anne of Temple Grafton in the novel is based loosely on young Juliet in the same play.

The idea for the death of Mopsa, the barmaid, came from an actual incident and a scene involving the suicide of a well-known Shakespeare character. On December 17, 1579, a Stratford spinster named Katherine Hamlet, who was carrying a milk pail, was found drowned in the icy Avon River. Residents debated whether this was in fact a suicide, which would have eliminated the young woman's claim to a Christian burial. Shakespeare later wrote of Ophelia's tragic "muddy death" in his play *Hamlet*.

Again I made use of historical record and a Shakespeare creation in Whittington, the novel's shepherd who served as the lovers' go-between. In 1601 Thomas Whittington, longtime Hathaway employee, left forty shillings to the poor in his will after his death. The Stratford record showed that Whittington gave the money for safekeeping "in the hand of Anne Shakespeare, wife unto Mr. Wm. Shakespeare." The connection between the old shepherd and Anne of

Shottery intrigued me. What was their relationship? I found it especially compelling that Shakespeare had an old shepherd make the moving speech about wild youth in act three of *The Winter's Tale*. It was the shepherd's lines that made me first think about writing this book:

> *"I would there were no age between ten and three-and-twenty, or that youth would sleep out the rest; for there is nothing in the between but getting wenches with child, wronging the ancientry, stealing, fighting . . ." [III.iii.60]*

As a final note, throughout *The Two Loves of Will Shakespeare* wherever poetry appears it is indeed the sonnets written by Shakespeare. I leave it up to the reader to discover more about the beauty and power of his words. As his publishers wrote in the preface to the *First Folio* of his plays, "Read him, therefore, and again and again. . . ."

Glossary

Bailiff, high bailiff: The mayor

Bandore: A lute-like instrument

"Black chaos come again": A reference to the idea that chaos follows loss of love

Blackguard: A thoroughly unprincipled person, a scoundrel

Bottom: Spirit

Cesspit: The hole in the ground beneath an outhouse used to collect refuse

Cittern: A guitar

Clinkered spirit: A first-rate spirit

Coif: A tight-fitting cap worn by women that was tied beneath the chin

Coz: Short for cousin, often used as a term of friendship

Dawcock: A silly fellow

Drabs: Harlots

Frumenty: Hot cereal made of cooked wheat and milk, broth, or water

Giglots: Wanton girls

Groat: A silver coin worth four pence

Gastful: Hideous

Guildhall: A large building used for aldermen meetings

"He made a scurvy face": He made a contorted, mean expression with his mouth.

Huzzah!: An expression meaning hurrah

Jerkin: A close-fitting, sleeveless jacket that was hip-length and often worn belted

Kirtle: A garment that women wore outside their dresses. Kirtles had two separate parts, a bodice and a skirt, and an opening in front.

Luce: A fish, a kind of pickerel

Mad wag: A crazy joker, a wild talker

Mummying: Acting or pretending

Nonny: A term of endearment

Plash of pond: A small place

"Quick . . . child brags in her belly": An unborn child has begun to "quicken" or move.

Recusant: Someone who refuses to give up prior faith, in this case, Catholicism

Robin Goodfellow: A fairy or trickster sometimes called Puck

Rough music: The tradition of playing loud instruments, banging on pans on the night of wedding for newlyweds

Sirrah!: An expression of derision

Small beer: Weak or diluted beer

"Speaks his part prately": Does a clever job

Stile: Steps that lead over a fence in a field

Stratum: Strategy

"The sweats": A disease that commonly afflicted adolescents as a fatal fever

Tom O'Bedlam: In 1547 King Henry VIII helped create Bethlehem Hospital in London as an asylum for the mentally deranged. It later became known as Bedlam Hospital, an institution with a brutal, inhumane reputation. The inmates were called "bedlam beggars" and were also known as "Tom O'Bedlams." Shakespeare referred to "Tom O'Bedlam" in several plays, including *King Lear*.

Wall of wattle and daub: Wall made of poles interwoven with slender reeds (wattle) and covered with a layer of clay or earth (daub)

Wedding banns: Public proclamations of names of newly engaged

"What bib!": What nonsense!

Wool brogging: Illegal wool selling or dealing without a proper license

Wonderful forward: Bold

"Worthless drevyll": An untrustworthy servant

"Wrabbed luck": Misfortune

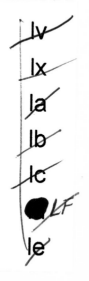